"I forbid you to keep that appointment."

Her teacher sounded angry. "You forbid me?" Amanda repeated incredulously. As he leaned back and regarded her, Amanda wanted to know what right Lewis had to forbid her, but she knew. If she was going to be a singer she was partly his creation, and he was fighting for his part in her.

"All right," she sighed, "I'll cancel the audition." Only then did she realize how tense Lewis had been.

"Good girl," was all he said, but as he passed he bent over to drop a seemingly careless kiss on the top of her head.

She sat motionless after he had gone, suddenly vitally aware of just why she felt so bound to follow any advice—or order—that Lewis cared to give!

Other titles by
MARY BURCHELL
IN HARLEQUIN ROMANCES

Other titles by
MARY BURCHELL
IN HARLEQUIN PRESENTS

Many of these titles are available at your local bookseller.

For a free catalogue listing all available Harlequin Romances,
send your name and address to:

HARLEQUIN READER SERVICE,
M.P.O. Box 707, Niagara Falls, N.Y. 14302
Canadian address: Stratford, Ontario, Canada N5A 6W2

Nightingales

by

MARY BURCHELL

Harlequin Books

TORONTO • LONDON • LOS ANGELES • AMSTERDAM
SYDNEY • HAMBURG • PARIS • STOCKHOLM • ATHENS • TOKYO

Original hardcover edition published in 1980
by Mills & Boon Limited

ISBN 0-373-02359-6

Harlequin edition published October 1980

CHAPTER ONE

'OH, Nan!' Amanda sniffed appreciatively as she came into the breakfast room of her brother's small hotel. 'How delicious your coffee always smells. And just look at the sunlight on that blossom——' she crossed the room to the deep bay window and looked out with pleasure on the untidy garden. 'It's the sort of day when you feel just anything might happen, isn't it?'

For a moment neither of the other two people in the room showed signs of pursuing this optimistic line of thought. Then her brother grinned and said, 'I presume you mean anything *nice* might happen?'

'Does anything nice ever happen around here?' his wife put in shortly. And Amanda swung round to exclaim reproachfully, 'Nan, you know it does!'

'For you perhaps.' Nan pushed back her still gleaming fair hair with both hands, and Amanda noticed for the first time that there were a few fine lines on that once smooth forehead.

'For all of us,' asserted Henry firmly. 'We balanced the books last month with even quite a bit in hand. We're over the hump so far as the winter off-season is concerned—and here's a letter from young Clive saying that school is super and do we feel like sending a small advance on his pocket money in view of the fact that he's come top in French!'

Nan laughed reluctantly, but she picked up the letter with a show of genuine interest, for if there was one thing in the world calculated to resign her to what she regarded as her rather unfair lot it was the existence of her nine-year-old son. Indeed, she immediately became absorbed in his schoolboy effusion to the exclusion of everything else, not even looking up when her husband pushed back his empty plate, got up from the table and limped out of the room.

It was Amanda who looked after him with a faint shadow now on the usual brightness of her face and an irrepressible tightening at the corners of her mouth. For although there were times when she felt desperately sorry for her lovely sister-in-law, there were other times—like now—when she could cheerfully have slapped her. Admittedly life had dealt Nan some cruel blows. But then that was a way life had; and Nan was not the only one in the family to have had to discover that sad truth.

Once, a few years ago, Amanda had ventured to point out that Henry too had had his share of ill luck. But Nan's face had hardened and she had replied with astonishing bitterness. 'It was Henry's own fault. He should never have gone on as a racing motorist once he was a married man. I begged him to give it up. There were half a dozen things he could have done then. He was young and brilliant and the fittest thing on earth. But he wouldn't listen to me.'

'But he let you follow *your* chosen career,' Amanda said, trying not to feel too resentful on her brother's behalf. 'He raised no objection to your going on with your training as a singer, did he?'

'Why should he?' was the scornful reply. '*I* wasn't risking my life. Just living in perpetual fear because he was risking his. He would say, "You have fun with your singing, darling, and I'll have fun with the cars." As though the two things were in any way comparable!'

'Nan, he wasn't indifferent to your anxiety. It was just that—oh, he was always car-crazy. Even when I was a little girl I knew that.'

'Yes——' suddenly Nan's voice was dejected rather than bitter. 'He didn't seem to be able to do anything about it. It was like a drug. Then when I found Clive was coming I hoped the responsibility of a child might make Henry give up racing. But there was no question of it. He was sweet to me about the new situation, as anxious as I was that I shouldn't abandon the career I was just starting. He would have given me anything—except peace of mind. No care or expense was too much to see that Clive was looked after perfectly so that I could be free. And then—the accident happened.'

'Oh, Nan——' Amanda had ached with sympathy for her sister-in-law at that moment. 'I can just imagine——'

'You can't imagine at all,' was the harsh rejoinder. 'You were just a kid at school, with an elder brother who had had an accident. I was his wife—the mother of a young child—with my life in ruins. For those first few months he just lay there like a log, and they told me he would never even walk again.'

'But he did!' Amanda protested, her voice thick in her throat with emotion. 'He did.'

'Oh, yes. That at least was granted to us.' Nan gave a short, not very pleasant laugh. 'But precious little else.' She was silent for a moment, as though contemplating again the depths of despair into which she had been thrust. Then she spoke again almost coldly. 'You know that was what really killed your father, don't you?'

'It was nothing of the kind!' Amanda spoke in pain and anger, her voice running up on to a high note of protest. 'Father had a poor heart condition for the last three years of his life.'

'And what do you suppose that sort of shock did for an elderly man with a poor heart condition?' replied Nan drily. 'I *saw* him when he stood beside Henry's bed and realised the truth—that he could hardly even move his head. You didn't. You were at boarding school. You were out of it all.'

'I know you carried the heaviest burden of us all, Nan,' Amanda said earnestly. 'Particularly as Mother had died the previous year. But *that* was what administered the first shock to Dad's weak heart, you know. You can't blame Henry for that.'

'I wasn't blaming him, exactly. At least, I don't think I was.' Nan shrugged and gave a slight wry smile. 'I suppose it's just that one can't help being bitter at times.'

'I do understand,' Amanda insisted eagerly. 'And I simply don't know what we should all have done without you.'

'Well, nor do I,' was the candid reply, but that time Nan's smile was kinder and had a hint of real humour in it. 'Anyway, I was glad when you came to live with us, Mandy—' she seldom used that affectionate form of Amanda's name, and it warmed Amanda's heart— 'don't ever think anything else, even when I'm in a foul temper. You're a good kid. I doubt if many young girls today would work the way you do. And at such dreary tasks too! Domestic chores are the end, so far as I'm concerned.'

'I really don't mind them,' Amanda declared. 'I like to see results for what I'm doing. And having our own small hotel is rather fun in some ways. Though, there again, so much depends on you,' she conceded generously. 'I daresay I do put in some hard work, and Henry is marvellous with the books and popular with all the guests. But without your fantastic cooking we wouldn't be building up such a reputation. We'd just be another average, prettily situated hotel.'

'Well—' at the end of that conversation Nan had touched Amanda's shoulder not unkindly, but she sighed too—'that's some consolation, anyway, when I recall my youthful visions of myself bowing from a stage or platform to a cheering audience, with my arms full of flowers.'

Nan seldom spoke now of her earlier musical aspirations. But whenever she did Amanda experienced an uneasy twinge of conscience; for this was the one subject on which she had felt bound to be less than candid with her sister-in-law. Here indeed she understood to the last degree Nan's sense of frustration und grievance. For what, Amanda asked herself, would *she* have felt if her singing lessons—those almost surreptitious singing lessons which meant so much to her—had had to come to an end?

Sometimes—on a bright, not too busy morning like this, for instance—she would allow herself to look back on what had happened, and even, with some trepidation, forward a little to what *might* happen.

Amanda had been twelve when her adored elder brother had married, and she had been immediately willing to love her new sister-in-law without a trace of jealousy. Nan had been so gay in those days. Gay and charming and talented. And if her career was hardly more than in the budding stages, to Amanda it seemed she was already a star. It had been wonderful to be a bridesmaid to this gorgeous creature and later a proud young aunt to Clive when he made his unexpected appearance in the second year of the marriage.

And then tragedy had struck—not once, but several times. First there had been the death of her mother, from pneumonia which followed with terrifying suddenness on a foolishly neglected cold.

Amanda had always loved both her parents dearly, but she had never been in any doubt which was the dominant one in the partnership. Energetic, slightly managing and infinitely capable, the older Mrs Lovett had directed, loved, guided and cossetted her husband and daughter. Both of them had tended to lean on her (as indeed she wanted them to do), her charming, not very forceful husband to a greater degree than the daughter who had in her own composition something of her mother's strength and energy. When she died so suddenly the shock to the very foundations of existence had been almost as painful as the grief and bewilderment which overwhelmed both father and daughter.

Amanda was young enough to rally and come to terms with a very different home situation, and during her school holidays she had done her best to be a prop and comfort to her father. But the core had gone out of existence for him. And when the other fearful shock of Henry's accident occurred, he seemed to give up even the wish to live and just faded out of a life which had ceased to be of much interest to him.

Without doubt it was Nan who had borne the brunt of the family tragedies in those early days. But presently Henry, with the determination, courage and sheer will-power which had made him such a brilliant racing driver, fought his way back to a certain degree of health. He had some capital left—though as always in these sad circumstances rather less than had been anticipated—and, after one or two attempts to carve out a new profession for himself, he sank almost everything he had in the purchase of a charming private hotel in one of the most attractive parts of Hampshire. Secluded enough to be appealing but sufficiently near to the main roads to be easily accessible, it offered at least a fifty-fifty chance of good development.

It was a gamble, of course. But then Henry was a gambler. He had been used to gambling with death in his time as a racing driver, and his incurable optimism carried him, and his family, through the first difficult years. Even optimism, however, would not have been enough if Nan had not proved herself to be, in addition to her other talents, a caterer with a touch of something like genius. Just as she had displayed style and charm and a sort of star quality in her early attempts at a public career, so she displayed the same qualities in the model kitchen which she insisted on having in their family hotel.

'Most singers are good cooks,' she had declared, with some truth, and she proceeded to prove the truth of this adage, at least so far as she herself was concerned. Today she could no longer lay much claim to being a singer, but she could certainly claim to be an outstanding cook, with a growing reputation in the country around and a capacity for astonishing the casual visitor.

When Amanda left school she almost automatically joined the family enterprise, carrying with her the one secret she could not disclose to Nan, of all people. But it is hard to tread upon one's dreams, particularly when one is young. So Amanda cherished her dreams, even if they sometimes had to be crowded into odd corners of her busy life.

It had been in her last year at school, just before her eighteenth birthday, that what she secretly thought of as The Discovery had been made. She had always enjoyed her school music lessons and had, for what that was worth, been a leading soprano in the school choir. The head of the music section happened to be not only a highly gifted woman but an ambitious and adventurous one as well. School concerts under her were neither conventional nor drably worthy. In with performances of the better known works for school choirs were mixed occasional modern works of genuine merit.

'Nothing trashy or trendy just because it happens to have been composed last year,' Miss Egerton once said to Amanda. 'Always remember there is no virtue in anything just because it is new, any more than just because it is old. Though works which have stood the test of time are likely to surpass those which are untried. New works can prove to be great discoveries or great bores. More frequently the latter, unfortunately,' she added drily. 'However, I propose to take a chance this time on Jerome Leydon's new cantata. You have heard of Jerome Leydon, of course?'

Amanda said, with comparative truth, that she had. By which she meant that the name was vaguely familiar to her, but if he had turned out to be a distinguished scientist or politician (if such there be) she would not have been in a position to query the statement.

'There is a beautiful little soprano solo in the work, and I propose to let you sing it,' Miss Egerton went on. 'It lies well for your voice and, if you work hard on it, you might make quite a success of it.'

So Amanda, who fell in love with the eminently singable air as soon as she heard it, worked hard;

and on the night of the concert she made more than 'quite a success' and was warmly congratulated by several parents. This was both comforting and encouraging since no one from her own family had been able to be present.

Afterwards, when audience and performers were being regaled with weakish coffee and the kind of conventional sandwiches which would never have found a place on any menu composed by Nan, a tall young man with untidy dark hair and unexpectedly blue eyes came up to her and said, 'You have a very unusual voice. Who taught you to sing?'

'Well—no one, in the sense of private singing lessons,' Amanda replied. 'I have piano lessons here at school, but I suppose any *singing* lessons would consist of what I've picked up at choir practice with Miss Egerton, our music teacher.'

'Then you must be a natural,' declared the young man, which Amanda found less than flattering since she had always understood a 'natural' to be only two removes from the village idiot.

'Vocally speaking, of course,' added the young man, evidently reading her thoughts, and he smiled suddenly with a brilliance which lit up his face to an almost startling degree. 'Have you any plans to have that voice trained? It's worth it, you know. So far it's a perfectly fresh, healthy organ which has had no harm done to it. There isn't much subtlety, of course, and there are virtually no nuances. If you take my advice——'

'Is there any special reason why I *should* take your advice?' interrupted Amanda, nettled by his assumption of authority towards the 'natural'.

'Only if you know what's good for you,' he replied, and again that brilliant smile flashed out. 'But I did

compose the air you sang and have some idea of how
it should go.'

'Oh!' she gasped. 'You mean you're Jerome Leydon? I'm terribly sorry. I had no idea——'

'No need to be sorry. My sister tells me I'm often
offensive when I'm laying down the law about my
own profession. I expect it's really I who should
apologise. But I'm not going to. Instead I'm going to
repeat—Have you any plans about having your voice
trained?'

Amanda shook her head slowly. 'It would—be
difficult,' she said in a low voice, for suddenly she
had remembered Nan.

'Aren't difficulties there to be overcome?' he challenged her bracingly. 'The artist who succeeds has
usually had to tackle a good many of them. Where
do you live?'

She told him, and he frowned consideringly and
finally said, 'You're quite near Austin Parva, then?'

'About three miles away. I sometimes cycle over
there when——'

'Oh, you cycle, do you? Come, that makes it
easier,' he interrupted with an air of arranging her
future for her. 'There's a very good organist and
choirmaster there at St Mary's. Do you know him?—
No?—Well, you might not. He's only recently
settled there. But he's already doing very fine work
with that choir. You'd better see if you can join, if
only in your school holidays. He might give you some
individual lessons, which would be very good for
you. Contact him when you're around there, and tell
him I sent you.'

And then he walked away, just exactly as though
he had some sort of right to advise—even order—her
what to do with her life.

Amanda, who was not at all the doormat type of girl, was faintly annoyed. But she would not have been human if she had not also been intrigued. To have an interest taken in her musical development by a real live composer—a composer moreover who had written the lovely air she had just sung with such good effect—was both flattering and exciting. If only there had not been the complication of Nan and her frustrated ambitions! For how could she, who had been so cruelly robbed of her own musical hopes, be expected to accept into her home circle someone who was striving to succeed where she had failed?

But Jerome Leydon had said that difficulties were there to be overcome. And, however little she felt inclined to take what had almost amounted to orders from him, what he had said had appealed strongly to Amanda's own innermost beliefs. What were challenges *for* if one did not respond to them?

It was some while before she was able to act on his advice—or her own inclinations. But, once her schooldays were over and she had settled into the routine of life in the family hotel, she began to look around for an opportunity to make some contact with St Mary's Church in Austin Parva. Though how she was to do this without offence or hurt to her sister-in-law she really could not imagine.

And then, nearly a year after she had finally left school, the opportunity arose, with almost dramatic simplicity and suddenness. Among the increasing number of 'locals' who dined frequently at the charming hotel where young Mrs Lovett put on such delicious and unusual menus was a Mrs Carter, the widow of a Lieutenant-Colonel. She was always most complimentary about Nan's culinary talents, but she was sometimes accompanied by her somewhat was-

pish sister, Miss Orton, who was much more sparing
with her praise. Miss Orton came from London and
felt in duty bound to show that her sights had been
set the higher for that fact. She seldom bestowed more
than the gracious smile of the *almost* (though not
completely) satisfied connoisseur on whatever was
set before her. But Nan—and Amanda too—had
learned not to be too deeply irritated by this sort of
patronage.

Mrs Carter enjoyed a degree of local chat and
gossip along with her after-dinner coffee and, if Nan
and Amanda were not too much engaged, would
draw them into conversation. It was on one of these
occasions that she observed,

'What a talented young woman you are, Mrs
Lovett! Not only do you turn out these delicious
meals, but someone was telling me that you *sing* as
well.'

Her admiring tone and choice of words immediately conjured up for Amanda a picture of Nan
turning the roast and singing the Mad Scene from
Lucia at one and the same time, and she had some
difficulty in suppressing a giggle. But Nan replied a
little sharply, 'Oh, I don't sing nowadays. There isn't
any time.'

'A pity,' observed Miss Orton judicially. 'Talents
should never be wasted. You should join the choir
at St Mary's at Austin Parva. The organist and choirmaster, Dr Elsworth, is exceptionally good, almost
worthy of a London appointment.'

Amanda was aware that her sister-in-law was
probably holding her breath and counting ten. So it
was tact as much as self-interest which prompted her
to say quickly, 'I've heard of him. Jerome Leydon
told me about him and said how gifted he was.'

'Jerome Leydon?' Miss Orton fixed her with an unbelieving stare. 'How did *you* come to discuss Dr Elsworth with Jerome Leydon?'

'He came to an end-of-term concert at my school,' explained Amanda lightly, as though Jerome Leydon were really nothing much in her young life. 'We'd sung a cantata of his and he spoke to—to some of us afterwards. And when I happened to say where I came from he mentioned Dr Elsworth and his remarkable work. He quite made me think I'd like to join that choir myself!'

'*You* would?' Nan laughed, but in a not unfriendly way since Amanda had contrived to put Miss Orton in her place in the nicest way possible. 'But have you got anything much of a voice?'

'Oh—well, I always warbled in the school choir, you know,' Amanda replied a trifle disingenuously. 'And I sometimes got a few solo lines.'

'I doubt,' observed Miss Orton majestically, 'if Dr Elsworth would be much interested in school choir warblers.'

'On the contrary, he might be glad to import a fresh young voice,' Nan remarked briskly. 'Most choirs tend to run a pretty high average age, don't they? I should go along and enquire, Amanda, if I were you. It could be rather fun for you. And goodness knows, you work hard enough here to merit some relaxation sometimes.'

So there it was! handed to her on a silver plate, by no less a person than Nan herself.

Amanda reflected on that fact with a sense of almost superstitious awe. And a few days later she said, 'You know, Nan, Austin Parva is only twenty minutes' run from where I'm going to order the honey. I think I *will* go and see if I can find this Dr

Elsworth they talk about. I always enjoyed choir singing at school and I quite like the idea of joining a good church choir.'

'Do,' replied Nan absently, for she was busily checking the contents of her store cupboard. 'You can but get a refusal. And if you were by any chance accepted it would be one in the eye for Miss Orton, which is quite a pleasant thought.'

Amanda laughed, made a cheerful thumbs-up sign, and mounted her bicycle with an air of setting off on a fairly unimportant quest instead of something which now made her heart beat with some excitement. During the ride she had time to experience several variations in the level of her hopes and expectations and, by the time she had dealt with the matter of the honey and gone on her way again, she had almost reached the point of deciding that she was wasting her time and entertaining inflated ideas about herself.

But as she rode into the delightful village of Austin Parva she told herself there was no harm in trying. And anyway, what was that bit about responding to a challenge?

There was no difficulty in identifying the church since it was the only one in the place—a beautiful late Norman structure of surprising size for such a comparatively small place. Amanda propped her bicycle against the churchyard wall and surveyed the scene with the pleased eye of a natural artist, and as she did so she became aware of the strains of an organ being played in the church.

It was almost like a stage cue. So she went slowly up the path to the deep porch, lifted the heavy latch of the door and, pushing open the door, stepped inside the church. Immediately she seemed surrounded by music. 'It was all round me and at the back of my neck as well,' she told Nan afterwards. 'My word, could that man play!'

Fascinated, she remained standing where she was, just inside the door, afraid that any movement or footstep of hers might disturb whoever was playing. The music was slightly familiar to her. Mozart, she decided. And then she recognised it for the beautiful 'Exsultate Jubilate', and at once a rising tide of excitement swamped her. It was, if she was not mistaken, the penultimate section, and must inevitably, if the player continued, end with the magnificent 'Alleluia'. If he did continue——

She took one or two deep, excited breaths and then, as the first note of the 'Alleluia' sounded she joined in, with a precision of 'attack' which even Miss Egerton would have approved.

The organist must have been startled, for there was the slightest hesitation in the rhythm of his playing, but then he went on. And Amanda went on singing. The most extraordinary feeling of elation took hold of her. She had never before sung in a place with such magnificent acoustics, and never before had she experienced this kind of support from a fellow performer. In some inexplicable way, it was like flying, and the sense of release and triumph which this gave her imparted just the right note of rapture to her singing.

So enthralled was she that when the music ceased she actually shook herself slightly, as though waking to reality again from a half-trance. At the same time a man's voice spoke with great clarity and some authority, and what he said was,

'You'd better come here and tell me who you are and where you learned to sing like that.'

Amanda came down the centre aisle then and, as she did so, a man got up from the organ bench and came down the few steps to her level. He was, she realised with surprise, quite young. Somehow she had visualised a Dr Elsworth who was a church organist and choirmaster as a rather venerable gentleman. He was not at all venerable. He was rather slightly built, had a pair of horn-rimmed spectacles pushed up on to his forehead and regarded her with an air of nervous attention which might have been shyness or short-sightedness, she decided.

'My name is Amanda Lovett,' she explained with a smile. 'Jerome Leydon told me about you and suggested I should come and see you, as I live near here. He thought I had quite—quite a respectable sort of voice and that you might be willing to let me join your choir.'

To her chagrin, he laughed unexpectedly at that, and she braced herself to receive what she thought was to be a scornful refusal. Nothing of the kind happened, however. What he said was, 'You can certainly join the choir—without further audition. But I must say that "respectable" is the last word I would have applied to that voice. "Seductive" would be more accurate.'

'I—beg your pardon!' Amanda drew herself up and gave this extraordinary choirmaster the chilliest glance she could achieve. 'I'm not that sort of girl at all.' And she turned away.

'Don't be silly,' said the authoritative voice behind her. 'It doesn't matter in the least what sort of girl you are. Nothing could be more boring or off the point. It's the *voice* I'm talking about. It has a most unusual quality. Where did you say you were trained?'

'I didn't,' replied Amanda, now beginning to feel rather silly. 'I haven't had any formal training, except in choir singing at school. Our teacher, Miss Egerton——'

Again he stopped her with that unexpected laugh.

'Good lord! Are you telling me that voice is the product of a schoolmistress and a girls' school choir? How intriguing!—Sit down——' he indicated the front pew beside which they were standing, and Amanda sank down on to the carved wooden seat and looked up enquiringly at the man who stood before her.

'Well, let's see what you're really like.' He brought down his spectacles from his forehead and this immediately imparted to him an air of authority to match his voice. At the same time, his look was not at all offensive—just a sort of general summing up, as though the girl in front of him were some sort of proposition he would have to assess.

Most men would have found Amanda an attractive proposition, it must be said, for she was one of those fortunate people gifted with very dark eyes but very fair skin and hair. No dazzled smile, however, greeted his closer view of her.

'You look healthy,' he observed, rather as a vet might comment on a horse whose teeth he was examining.

'Well, I am—if that's important,' Amanda retorted crisply.

'It's of paramount importance,' he replied, unruffled. 'The degree of stamina and vitality required by a singer is comparable to that required by a first class boxer.'

'You're speaking of a professional singer, of course?'

'Of what else were we talking? And what would you mean by an *un*professional singer, for heaven's sake?'

'Well—' she was slightly confused by this challenge—'I suppose I was thinking in terms of an amateur singer. One who——'

'I'm not interested in amateur singers,' he interrupted coldly. 'Every member of my choir is expected to work with the devotion and application of someone who regards singing as a professional job. There's no room for anyone who's just playing at it. That's why I get results.'

'I see.' Amanda spoke more meekly than she had intended. 'Then I doubt if I'm going to be of much use to you. Not because I'm not sufficiently interested and not because I disagree with anything you've said. But it's just a matter of the sheer time available.'

'What do you do with your evenings?' he enquired. 'Waste them with some silly young attachment who wants all your spare time and isn't even serious?' He glanced disparagingly at her bare left hand and then back at her face.

'No. I have no attachment, as it happens, either silly or otherwise. But I work in the small family hotel which belongs to my brother and sister-in-law, and evenings are our busy times. Sundays are an exception. That's why I thought I might be all right in a church choir. And I could certainly get away on one other evening a week—when I suppose you have choir practice.'

'What about lessons?'

'Lessons?'

'Individual lessons,' he amplified a trifle impatiently. 'You're going to need those if you're to develop your full potential. What else did you think?'

She had not, of course, really thought anything else at all. She had just wanted to *sing*. How far she might follow through from there she had no idea at the moment.

'I hadn't thought about it in detail,' she confessed. 'I just thought of joining a choir, and when I was at school——'

'Well, you're not at school now!' he almost shouted at her. 'Stop talking like a child.' And he swung from her to take two or three impatient steps before he turned and came back to her. 'Listen, I'm not going to give you an inflated idea of yourself. You have a very good voice, if I'm not much mistaken, and quite a lot of natural talent—which happens sometimes. But none of that is worth anything unless you're prepared to work. I'd like to hear you in something else before I say more. Do you sing anything operatic?'

Amanda shook her head doubtfully, and then said hesitantly, 'Would you call "Divinités du Styx" from Gluck's *Alceste* operatic?'

'I would,' he replied grimly, and his withering glance informed her that she had made another bad slip by even querying such a thing. 'Do you sing it in the original key?'

'Yes,' she stated boldly, having no idea whether she did or not, but determined not to show any further indecision.

'Come and stand over here.'

She followed him until she stood quite near the organ, when he imperiously waved her a little further off and said, 'You can give the climax all the power you've got. I'd like to hear the actual size of the voice.'

With nervous haste Amanda mentally reviewed the aria, trying to decide exactly where the climax came. Then, just as though someone had literally prompted her, she thought, 'She's imploring the gods of the underworld to restore the man she loves. The music grows quite naturally with the strength of her appeal.'

There was something strange and awesome about standing there in a church built hundreds of years ago to the glory of God, and singing an impassioned appeal to the pagan gods of the underworld. On the one hand a tremendous depth of feeling, on the other the cool classical line of the music. She forgot about Dr Elsworth or what he might have ultimately to say about her voice. She was one with the loving woman she was portraying.

But she remembered him as she finished the aria and turned round quickly to look at him. He was still sitting at the organ, but *he* had turned to regard *her* with a sort of amused incredulity.

'Out of a girls' school choir!' he said, as though commenting to someone other than Amanda herself. 'Well, we'll have to see what we can do with that voice. It's much too good to go to waste. You'll have to explain to your brother and sister-in-law that——'

'Oh, I couldn't tell *them* about it!' Amanda insisted in some agitation. 'At least, not her.'

'Why not?' He sounded as though he were preserving his patience with some difficulty.

'Well, you see——' with great earnestness and in some detail Amanda explained about Nan and her early ambitions. She thought he was listening with some sympathy, but at the end he said,

'It seems a great lot of nonsense to me.'

'Oh, it's not! It's a question of people's happiness. The happiness of people I'm very fond of, incidentally. It would *kill* Nan to have someone right in the family succeed where she'd failed through no fault of her own.'

'People aren't killed so easily,' he replied callously. 'And don't talk so confidently of your success. You haven't even started. However, we'll take this silly family secret into consideration if you think it important. Now, how much time would you be able to devote to all this? You say you can get away on Sundays and one other evening. Wednesday evening is when we have choir practice. If you were vague at home about the actual timetable, you could get in one lesson before the choir practice, and another one some time on Sunday, either before or after evening service. How about home practising?'

'I could manage fairly well.' Insensibly she found herself falling in with his imperious calculations. 'Nan's piano is stored away in one of the unused rooms of the house. A remote room, as it happens. I think—' her voice dropped a compassionate note or two—'she just couldn't bear to have it around.'

'Very likely,' he agreed with shocking indifference. 'Well, that's fortunate. The arrangements aren't ideal, but we might try them for six months and see how you get on.'

'There's just one other thing!' Amanda blushed furiously as she remembered an absolute essential which had not yet been discussed. 'I don't know whether I have enough—I mean, would the lessons be very expensive?'

'No. They would be free.'

'Free? Oh, but I couldn't allow that! You don't even know me. It—it would be a sort of imposition.'

'Not since I do it by my own choice. And I assure you that if I find at the end of six months that you're not worthy of my teaching or time, I shall have no hesitation in terminating the arrangement.'

'Then it's—an experiment?' She smiled slowly and, though she did not know it, very beautifully. For gradually it was dawning on her that perhaps dreams did sometimes come true.

'It's an experiment,' he confirmed. 'For six months only. And then we will review the position in the light of your progress—or lack of it.' Then he added briskly, 'Today is Monday. I'll expect you in the church schoolroom next door at five o'clock on Wednesday. Without fail.'

'Without fail,' she promised him jubilantly.

And all the way home, as she bowled along on her bicycle, she kept repeating to herself, 'Without fail—without fail.' As though, in some magical way, that would ensure the success of this most romantic venture.

To her relief, explanations at home proved to be a good deal easier than she had anticipated. Nan seemed amused rather than curious when Amanda explained that Dr Elsworth had somewhat informally auditioned her and decided that she was acceptable in his choir. And even over the matter of arranging the times when Amanda could be missing, Nan just said, 'You *are* taking it all very seriously, aren't you?'

'Well, he seems pretty strict,' Amanda replied. 'He implied that it was something of an honour to be

accepted and that he expected people to toe the line.
—*His* line.'

'We must let Miss Orton know presently,' observed Nan with some satisfaction. And that was all.

So the six months' trial began the following Wednesday, with a rather painful first lesson during which Amanda was given to understand that she had almost everything to learn. But even on that first harrowing occasion she already had some inkling of the sheer fascination of the struggle to perfect any form of art. As a teacher Dr Elsworth was not conspicuous for his patience. But what he did have was a talent, amounting almost to genius, for explaining exactly what he wanted and, provided one were musically intelligent, how this might be achieved.

'I don't suffer fools gladly. No teacher worth his salt does,' he informed her at an early stage, and she took the hint and made it her business to prepare herself thoroughly for her lessons. Even so, of course, she tripped up sometimes and she thought him unkind in his criticism and arrogant in his demands.

'You remind me of Jerome Leydon,' she told him rather resentfully on one of these occasions.

'I do?' He looked astonished and not particularly pleased. 'He wouldn't be flattered to hear you say that.'

'Why not?' she could not resist asking.

Unexpectedly he laughed and pushed up his glasses on his forehead. 'He's usually rated as something in the nature of a heart-throb. We were in music college together and he was definitely the star of that period. Why do I remind you of him?'

'You're both so—so sure of yourselves. So determined to order one's existence.'

'When did he try to order your existence?' There was a touch of genuine curiosity in the query.

'He practically ordered me to come and see you and ask to be admitted to your choir and perhaps have lessons with you.'

'You don't say?' Lewis Elsworth looked amused. (She had discovered that his name was Lewis from a church notice, but she had never heard anyone address him as such.) 'Well, for that at any rate we must be grateful,' he added—a little enigmatically, she thought. 'Shall we try that last bit again?'

Looking back now, Amanda saw those first six months through a haze of increasing knowledge and delight—punctuated, admittedly, from time to time by explosions of wrath on his part and near-despair on hers. But, on balance, they were extraordinarily happy months and, at the end of them, there was no question of the experiment finishing there.

'As I said all along, the conditions are not ideal,' he told her. 'But conditions seldom are, and you're not doing at all badly.'

This was reasonably high praise from him and she was happy. However, she felt bound to bring up the question of fees once more.

'Don't be silly,' he said. And then, with a smile of rare indulgence, 'You can pay me after your first Covent Garden engagement.'

'Do you really *think* that one day——'

'That was a joke,' he interrupted curtly. 'And not a specially good one either. But if you work hard there's no saying what might happen—one day.'

So she went on working hard. She had been doing so now for close on two years. And from time to time she told herself that anything might happen. Though what she meant by that she was not quite sure. Nor could she imagine what effect the unspecified 'anything' might have on her life and family.

On Nan, for instance. Suppose she had some enormous stroke of luck?—met someone who could put her on the road to success—won some contest which brought her publicity—how would that affect Nan? The thought of her sister-in-law was always inextricably mixed in with any hopes or ambitions she might entertain on her own behalf. Even today, when she had thoughtlessly declared it was the kind of day when anything might happen, Nan's quick, discontented reaction had immediately made her feel guilty.

But as the day went on its reassuringly uneventful way her thoughts veered away from the problem of Nan, and by the time she went to her room to change, late in the afternoon, she was already thinking more of her coming lesson and choir practice than of any family problems.

Just as she was ready to go down she heard a car drive up outside and, glancing from the window, she saw a good-looking woman step out of a very handsome Daimler. She drew her mink jacket round her, glanced up at the sign which hung outside the hotel and called to someone still in the car,

'It's called The Nightingale. Isn't that charmingly appropriate?'

Amanda did not hear the reply. But, catching up her coat, she ran down the back staircase to alert either Nan or Henry to the arrival of this distinguished-looking visitor, before going on her own way to Austin Parva.

There was no one in the family sitting-room when she came in but, before she could go in further search of her brother or sister-in-law, the door from the main part of the hotel opened and Nan came in. A flushed, bright-eyed, strangely lovely-looking Nan, who pushed the door to behind her and leaned against it, catching her breath in such obvious agitation that Amanda exclaimed involuntarily.

'Nan! What is it?'

'You can't imagine who's just arrived!—Here!—in our ordinary little hotel. Oh, what would I have given to have this happen ten years ago!'

'But who is she? I did see a gorgeous-looking car draw up, but——'

'*She?*' Nan's tone dismissed the unknown 'she' as almost negligible. 'She's just his wife—though a singer in her own right, of course. It's he who matters. The man who's just come into *our* hotel is Oscar Warrender.'

And if Nan had been announcing the arrival of the Archangel Gabriel she could not, Amanda thought, have sounded more awed or excited.

CHAPTER TWO

'Oscar Warrender?' Amanda repeated incredulously. 'Do you mean *the* Oscar Warrender?'

'There's only one,' replied Nan. 'And he's come ten years too late,' she added bitterly.

'What do you mean by that?' In her surprise and excitement, Amanda had for once forgotten Nan's lost ambitions.

'They say he's always on the lookout for new vocal talent. Ten years ago I'd have managed somehow to make him listen to me—take me seriously. I was part of his world of music then, however young and unimportant. I would have gatecrashed in some way. Now—' Nan glanced round as though assessing her surroundings almost with hatred—'now I'm the landlady of a small hotel, and the most I can do is go and serve tea to him and his wife.'

'I'll go if you like,' Amanda offered, a quiver of uncontrollable eagerness in her voice. 'Let me. I'd like to.'

'No. It's time you were off to your choir practice, isn't it? Besides—' Nan gave a half contemptuous little shrug—'at least I'll have a word with him, if it's only, "Would you like some more hot water, sir?"'

'Then just let me carry somthing in,' pleaded Amanda. 'One doesn't often have a chance to brush shoulders with a celebrity. Two celebrities, come to that. She's famous in her own right, isn't she? Let me see—what's her name? Her professional name,

31

I mean. Anthea—Anthea "something".'

'She was Anthea Benton before he married her. He discovered *her* in some romantic circumstances or other. She's usually known as Anthea Warrender now.—All right, take in the scones and cream and jam. I'll bring along the tea in a minute or two. But —' Nan glanced sharply at Amanda—'don't say anything gushing or unprofessional, will you? We needn't seem to be country bumpkins, even if we are now.'

'Of course not!' Amanda had already flung down her coat and picked up a tray on to which she piled several of the delectable things which her sister-in-law considered essential to a proper tea. Then, her heart beating with excitement, she went through to the pleasant dining-room at the front of the house.

They were both looking out at the garden, Warrender standing with his back to the room and his wife sitting at the table in the bay window. She turned her head immediately at the sound of Amanda's entry and exclaimed, 'What an enchanting place you have here!'

'It is rather nice, isn't it?' Amanda smiled irresistibly because it was difficult not to smile when Anthea Warrender looked so genuinely interested and friendly. 'My brother and sister-in-law run the place and I help out. I enjoy it, even though it's quite hard work.'

'It must be! I like the name of the hotel too.'

'Yes? I heard you say that "The Nightingale" was charmingly appropriate. I wondered why.'

'Oh, dear!' Anthea Warrender looked both amused and slightly shocked. 'Did my voice actually penetrate into the house? I had no idea I spoke so loudly.'

'It's that technique which projects to the last row of the gallery,' observed the man, turning round from the window, and Amanda had her first, and overwhelming, impression of the famous conductor. He was smiling slightly, so that she found him less formidable than his reputation had led her to expect, but there was no question about his air of authority.

Warrender must, she supposed, be in his late forties—possibly early fifties—but he gave the impression of such vitality and inner strength that it would have been hard to put an age to him. Like many fair-haired men, he seemed scarcely to have greyed at all, the touch of silver at the temples merely adding an almost youthful brightness to the smooth hair.

'She doesn't understand the allusion,' Anthea Warrender said. 'We're stage people,' she explained in a friendly way, 'and we tend to speak in theatre terms.'

'I realise that,' Amanda said shyly but with an air of almost naïve interest which would have been engaging to the most modest of people. 'I—know who you are.'

'Really?' Anthea seemed amused and surprised. 'Did you recogise us when you came into the room, then?'

'No. My sister-in-law recognised you and told me you were here. And I begged to be allowed to bring in some of your tea things and see you for myself,' Amanda admitted with charming candour.

Both the Warrenders laughed at that, and he said, 'There's fame for you! But that still doesn't tell you why my wife found The Nightingale an appropriate name. I suppose you might say we're in search of a nightingale. In other words, there's supposed to be a promising young singer in the district. She'll probably prove to be nothing of the kind, of course,' he added in cynical parenthesis. 'They nearly always do. But we'll take the chance of hearing her just the same. Do you know a place near here called Austin Parva?'

'Yes.' Amanda swallowed hard and tried to stifle a slight gasp. 'It's about three miles from here. It—it has a rather beautiful church. L—late Norman.'

'And a very good choir and choirmaster, I'm told.' The conductor glanced at her with a touch of interest, and she had the most extraordinary conviction that he *knew* she was breathless with excitement.

'Dr Elsworth—yes. He's very good.'

But at that moment Nan came in, looking admirably calm and collected, and she said, 'It's time you were off, Mandy, if you're not going to be late for choir practice.'

Amanda guessed her sister-in-law had thought up that opening remark with the intention of drawing a word or two about singing from her two visitors. So she replied quickly, 'Yes. I'm—just going.'

'To Austin Parva?' enquired Oscar Warrender coolly. 'Then we won't keep you. Go along. You mustn't be late.'

And, desperately tempted though she was to linger for a few moments longer, Amanda took her departure immediately, aware with absolute certainty that when Oscar Warrender said, 'Go along,' one went.

As she glanced at the hall clock she realised that she could not fail to be late for her lesson, a circumstance which would ordinarily have reduced her to agitated dismay. But the recent encounter, and the possibility implicit in what Warrender had told her, combined to make everything else seem almost unimportant.

Almost—but not quite. For even in her euphoric state she remembered the one other time she had been late for a lesson, and the recollection set her off pedalling madly in the hope of making up for lost time. Even so, she *was* late and rather breathless as she finally entered the church schoolroom, where her lessons usually took place.

Lewis Elsworth was already sitting at the piano, running his hands over the keys, and he said without looking up, 'You're late.'

Unusual rebellion rose in Amanda at that tone and, to her own surprise, she heard herself say, 'I know. I'm sorry. I was talking to Oscar Warrender.'

It was a wonderful comeback, and she was pleased to see that it shook him. He struck a discord on the piano and turned to look at her in the most gratifying surprise.

'Oscar Warrender? What's he doing round here?'

'I think—I'm not quite sure, but I think he may be coming to Austin Parva this evening. He seems to have heard of you and your choir——'

'From whom?' he interrupted quickly.

'I don't know. Would it perhaps be from Jerome Leydon? They might know each other, I suppose.'

'Yes, they probably do. Leydon gets around to most places—and people—of importance.' That was said without rancour, Amanda realised. 'But how did *you* come to be talking to Warrender?'

'He and his wife—Anthea Benton, you know—they both came into the hotel for tea and—and I served them. At least, I managed to take in some of the tea things.'

'And told him you sang in the choir? At which he said, "God, you're the soprano we've been looking for!" I suppose.'

'Nothing so silly and amateur,' she retorted crisply. 'On the contrary, *he* offered the information that they were in the district because they'd heard about you and your choir. And he also said——' She stopped, suddenly ashamed of her own eagerness to assign to herself those magic words about a promising soprano.

'Yes?' He glanced at her curiously.

'Nothing. My sister-in-law came in then and said it was time I went off to choir practice. She still thinks that's all I do when I come here on Wednesdays. So I had to agree with her and leave at that point. Even so, I'm late and I apologise.'

'It's all right,' he said unexpectedly. 'I'd have lingered too in those circumstances, I think. Oscar Warrender, hm? He didn't say anything about——? Well, it doesn't matter. We'll get on with the lesson now.'

So they got on with the lesson and, with a tremendous effort, Amanda managed to put the Warrenders sufficiently far into the back of her mind to give ninety per cent of her attention to what she was doing. But an odd thing happened. For the first time since she had known him, Lewis Elsworth failed to note a minor mistake on her part, and it occurred to her that he too seemed to have only ninety per cent of his attention on the lesson.

Towards the end of the session he said, almost casually, 'I think we might have you sing a solo after Evensong on Sunday. The congregation like that from time to time. How about "Hear ye, Israel"? We might run through it now. It's some time since you studied it.'

'Yes,' said Amanda, and that was all. But she realised that Lewis Elsworth meant her to sing 'Hear ye, Israel' if Warrender came into the church that evening, and to sing it to the best of her ability.

They went through it, with only one stop for a slight correction in the repeat of the main theme. Then he said, 'Yes, that will do,' and her lesson was over.

Usually at this point, when he went back to his own house at the other end of the village, Amanda went to see a fellow member of the choir with whom she had become friendly. But on this occasion, when he had departed, she decided that she must be alone for a short while, if only to put her thoughts in order and her feelings under control. So she went across to the church.

She hardly ever lifted the heavy latch of the church door without recalling briefly that first time when she had come in to hear Lewis Elsworth playing and stayed to sing for him. This evening, however, she was so deeply absorbed in her own thoughts that she just slipped into the church quietly and sat down at the very back.

For the first few minutes she thought she was the only person in the place. Then she heard the footsteps of someone who was walking slowly round near the altar. There was nothing unusual about this. The church was of sufficient beauty and historical interest to attract the occasional tourist. And she continued to sit there, her head bent over her copy of *Elijah*, undisturbed by the presence of any casual stranger. Until a man emerged from one of the side aisles, walked up to where she was sitting and said, 'Hello. I wondered if I might find you here.'

Amanda raised her head and was astonished to find Jerome Leydon standing in front of her.

'Why—hello!' Both surprise and pleasure imparted unusual warmth to her tone. 'What are you doing here?'

'I'm staying about twelve miles away with my sister. She has a house at Wetherton.'

'Is that the sister who says you're often offensive when you start laying down the law about your profession?' Amanda asked with a sudden mischievous smile.

'She does, as a matter of fact. But how did you know?' He sat down beside her, looking amused in his turn.

'You told me she did, the first time I ever met you. At the school concert when you heard me sing——'

'The first time I heard you sing,' he amended.

'The only time, surely?' she looked surprised.

'No. I've heard you twice since then,' he informed her. 'I made it my business to do so. I wanted to hear how you were developing. So twice, when I was staying with Diana, I came over here and slipped in at the back to listen for myself. You're doing well, aren't you?'

'I should like to think so,' Amanda said slowly.

'You mean old Lewis isn't exactly lavish with his praise?'

For some inexplicable reason she was faintly annoyed at hearing her teacher described as 'old Lewis'.

'He's a marvellous teacher,' she said a little curtly,

'and doesn't, I suppose, want to make the mistake of giving me inflated ideas about myself.'

'I bet he doesn't!' Jerome Leydon laughed with genuine amusement. 'But, at the risk of doing that very thing, I'm going to tell you *I* thought so well of you that I persuaded someone pretty influential to come and hear you tonight.'

'Oscar Warrender?' she said, just below her breath.

'Yes. How did you know?' He was not entirely pleased, she saw, to have his surprise anticipated, so she quickly explained about the Warrenders' visit to The Nightingale and added.

'I can't tell you how grateful I am to you for arranging this. How on earth did you do it?'

'I know the Warrenders quite well,' he explained. 'Anthea is a darling. And as for him—well, he's immensely knowledgeable, of course.'

'But not exactly a darling?' she suggested shrewdly.

'Hm—' he smiled reflectively—'disgruntled prima donnas have been known to describe him as a monster, I believe. But he has a sort of arrogant charm, if you like that sort of thing. I mentioned you to him some time ago, but he showed very little interest. Then, when I heard you again about a month ago, I told Warrender once more that he should hear you and, rather to my surprise, he asked whether Lewis Elsworth were the choirmaster down here and agreed that he and Anthea would make it their business to be in the district and hear you.'

'Then they're coming here this evening?'

'They're coming here this evening. Does it make you nervous to know about it beforehand?'

'Not paralysingly nervous,' said Amanda slowly.

'Just on my mettle, you know. I'd rather know in advance, as a matter of fact. It will make me doubly careful and eager to do my best.'

'Good girl!' He patted her shoulder lightly. 'You know, I was interested in you from the beginning. There's something quite special about you—about your voice. Do you ever come up to London?'

'Not very often. Sometimes, of course.'

'Warrender is conducting at the Festival Hall next Monday. Will you come up and have dinner with me and I'll take you on to the concert? Would you like that?'

'I'd *love* it!' exclaimed Amanda breathlessly. 'I'll have to see about last train times, though, because——'

'No problem. I'll drive you back and go on and spend the night at my sister's. Have you ever heard Warrender conduct?'

Amanda shook her head, her eyes wide with gratitude and admiration for anyone who could pull such important strings with such casual skill.

'Then you have quite an experience coming to you!' He got up with that brilliant smile she remembered so well from their first meeting. 'Anthea is singing too. The Letter Scene from *Eugene Onegin* and something else—I'm not quite sure what. I must go now. I expect you want to do a bit of last-minute revision. What are you singing, by the way? For I presume it's not going to be all choral work.'

She held out the music to him without comment.

'"Hear ye, Israel"? Good choice,' he approved. 'Give it a touch of drama. That appeals to Warrender. And after all, you *are* a celestial being addressing the Tribes of Israel on behalf of God. I'll see you later.' And, with a smile, he raised his hand in a gesture of farewell and went away out of the church.

One or two other members of the choir began to drift in now, and casual greetings were exchanged. Then presently Lewis Elsworth made his entrance and everyone, figuratively speaking, sprang to attention.

He glanced round, made no reference to the fact that this might prove to be a rather special evening and merely said, 'Everyone feeling on top form?— Good. I want the very best out of you for once.'

'When did he ever want anything less?' murmured the soprano beside Amanda. And one of the cheekiest, and most angelic-looking, of the choirboys volunteered the information, 'I think my voice is beginning to break, sir.'

'Well, don't let it do so until tomorrow morning,' was the dry retort. And the practice session began.

It was not until halfway through that Amanda saw the church door open and three people come quietly in and sit down at the back. There was a certain amount of shadow where they were sitting, but she knew instantly that they were the Warrenders and Jerome Leydon.

Lewis Elsworth must have seen them too, she supposed. But he remained so completely calm and unmoved that she felt her own quivering nerves grow quieter. Then he said,

'All right, the rest of you can take a breather. Amanda, we'll try your solo, shall we?'

'Yes, Dr Elsworth.'

She smiled back at him as though all she asked was to be an angel announcing God's purpose. And indeed Jerome Leydon's words came back to her with such force that she was suddenly able to visualise the scene and herself the centre of it.

'Hear ye, Israel!' she announced in tones of radiant authority, and a little tremor of response seemed to pass through everyone in the choir stalls. Whether the same effect reached to the back of the church she could not tell. She only knew that this was *her* moment, and if she had not actually got the Tribes of Israel in thrall, she was doing the best she could with the choir and, perhaps, the three important visitors at the back of the church.

When the last silvery note had floated up into the shadows of the roof, Amanda glanced across at Lewis Elsworth. For, in that moment, it was his reaction which suddenly seemed to be of most importance. This was just as well, for no one came rushing forward from the back of the church to exclaim, 'That's a voice in a thousand!' or even, 'Where have you been hiding in the last few years?'

Her teacher merely nodded to her and smiled, and she knew she had done well. Then, as she sat down again, one of the older tenors leaned forward and said, 'Well done! That's certainly your party piece, my girl. Never heard it better sung by an amateur.'

She smiled too then and felt satisfied.

The three visitors remained during the rest of the evening practice and only when the members of the choir were finally dispersing did they come forward. Even then they paused at intervals, as though to examine and admire various features of interest in the church. They were obviously, Amanda realised, waiting until most of the others should have gone and there would be a chance to speak to the choir-master on his own.

She stood where she was, a little undecided what to do next. Then, as the group came abreast of her, Warrender simply said, 'Very good. Go on working.'

And he went on to Lewis Elsworth, whom he immediately engaged in conversation.

Anthea paused a little longer and said warmly, 'You sing very beautifully. And "Hear ye, Israel" is a pretty stiff test of one's technique. You need a lot of vocal security for those high entries.'

'But it's a wonderful feeling when you bring them off, isn't it?' replied Amanda impulsively.

'Yes, it's a wonderful feeling,' Anthea agreed with a smile. 'I think my husband was impressed.'

But evidently it was not her way to enlarge too much on her husband's brief comments. She gave Amanda a friendly little nod but, when Jerome Leydon called to her to come and look at something he was examining, she went at once.

Looking round, Amanda saw that her teacher and Oscar Warrender were making their way towards the door leading to the changing rooms and the vicar's office. They were deep in conversation, quite unaware of her or anyone else, and hardly realising what she was doing, she followed them at a little distance.

As they entered the vicar's office she heard Lewis Elsworth say, 'She's good, isn't she?'

'She's quite unusually good,' replied the cool, incisive tones of the conductor. 'If she works hard with you for another year she'll be much better still. But it was not only about the girl I wanted to speak to you. As you know——'

And then at that point Lewis Elsworth came and pushed the door shut, and the mortified Amanda suddenly became aware of the fact that she had been most shamelessly eavesdropping. Whether Lewis Elsworth had realised this or not she could not tell, but she positively slunk away back into the church, thankful that there was no one near her to notice her deep flush.

Embarrassed as she was, she would have taken herself off home by now, but Anthea Warrender came up to her and said, 'I hear you're coming to our concert next week. Jerome must bring you round to see us afterwards.'

'Thank you very much. I—I'd like that immensely.'

'Did Sir Oscar say anything further to you about your singing?' Jerome Leydon asked with an air of friendly curiosity.

'No. I—' Amanda cleared her throat—'heard him say to Dr Elsworth that my voice was good and that I should be even better after another year with him.'

'Well, that's true, of course,' Anthea remarked. 'He isn't a man of many words, you know, particularly in the early days of a career.'

'*I* should have thought she was ready for something more than choir singing and weekly lessons,' Jerome Leydon said impatiently. 'Warrender is almost *over*-careful about young voices in my view.'

Anthea looked amused rather than offended by this and said mildly, 'He has a reputation for knowing quite a bit about the subject, you know.'

'All right.' Leydon laughed a little vexedly. 'I stand corrected. Will you be coming by train on Monday—Amanda?' He hesitated, but only for a second, before using her first name. 'Because if so I'll meet you at Waterloo. There's a good train which gets in about six. If you can catch that I'll meet you at the barrier, and we can dine at the Hall. That will avoid any rush.'

'Thank you. It sounds lovely,' said Amanda.

And to her it certainly did.

Then she bade them goodnight and went out into the gathering dusk. She would have liked to have a further word with her teacher, but he was still closeted with Oscar Warrender. So she mounted her bicycle and rode off home, wondering now what she was going to say to Nan.

'Did they turn up at the church?' her sister-in-law wanted to know as soon as she came in. And then, as Amanda nodded, 'What on earth could he find to interest him in a church choir?'

'It's an exceptionally good one and very well trained,' Amanda explained, with an air of candour of which she was slightly ashamed. 'Sir Oscar was talking quite animatedly to Dr Elsworth when I left.'

Nan bit her lip thoughtfully. Then she laughed suddenly and said, 'Well, Mandy, you did better than I did. At least you can say you once sang for Oscar Warrender, even if only as an unimportant member of a church choir.'

Amanda laughed in her turn, rather uncomfortably, and then said quickly, 'Something else rather exciting happened. Jerome Leydon turned up. Apparently he has a sister living quite near here. He remembered me from that time at school and we got talking afterwards. And—and when he found I'd never heard either of the Warrenders he just couldn't believe it. He said they were both going to be in a concert at the Festival Hall next Monday and —imagine!—he offered to take me. What do you think of that?'

'That some people have all the luck,' retorted Nan with a slight grimace. 'You accepted, of course?'

'Of course! You don't refuse a Warrender concert if it's tossed into your lap. He even said he would drive me home, so that I needn't worry about train times.'

'Fast worker,' commented Nan, looking at Amanda with some interest. 'Is he—smitten?'

'Oh, I don't think so. He didn't make passes, if that's what you mean. I think he was just intrigued to find I was thrilled by the Warrenders without having ever heard them. Or perhaps his regular girl had stood him up and he happened to have the extra ticket.'

'Perhaps.' Nan yawned suddenly. 'Well, I'm going to bed. It's been quite a day. I'll see you get away in good time on Monday. It's nice for you to have a treat for once.'

'Oh, Nan!' Unexpectedly Amanda flung her arms round her sister-in-law, in an access of gratitude, excitement and an obscure sort of guilt.

'What's this in aid of?' Nan asked with some amusement.

'Oh—just that you're a dear not to raise any objections, and to be glad that I'm having a treat.'

'Well, I have my faults—' Nan brushed a careless kiss across Amanda's cheek—'but I'm not a bitch about other people's good fortune—yet. I hope I never shall be.'

And, on that oddly prophetic utterance, she went off to bed.

It was not, of course, until the following Sunday that Amanda had a chance to discuss the Warrenders' visit with her teacher. And when they did meet it was he who spoke first.

'Why did Jerome Leydon want to hang around the other evening?' was what he said.

'*Hang around?*' Her tone was indignant. 'He didn't

hang around any more than anyone else did. I suppose he was interested to find out for himself what I sounded like.'

'I suppose he was.' Lewis Elsworth looked at her reflectively.

'Is there anything against that?' she asked shortly.

'I don't know,' was the unexpected reply. 'Our Jerome has been going off on a rather unexpected tack recently. He seems to have lost his taste for serious composing and is beginning to make quite a name for himself in much lighter stuff. Catchy and not without style and popular attraction, but meretricious. Good luck to him—so long as he doesn't try to involve you in it.'

'There's no question of such a thing!'

'Did he say as much?'

'No, of course not. We never even discussed my future beyond——' she stopped suddenly.

'Beyond what?' he wanted to know.

'Oh, it was nothing,' she exclaimed impatiently. 'Just that he said something about Sir Oscar being almost too careful about young singers and that he would have thought I was already a bit beyond choir singing and—and weekly singing lessons.'

'Charming,' observed her teacher drily. 'Did he add that he would like you to meet Max Arrowsmith and have a talk?'

'No.' Amanda shook her head. 'He never mentioned any such name. Who is Max Arrowsmith, anyway?'

'A considerable power in the world of light entertainment, and much in Jerome Leydon's pocket at the present time.'

'Well, that may be quite true, but absolutely no

mention was made of him. And now what I really
want to know is what Sir Oscar had to say about my
singing.'

'He was impressed,' was the cautious reply. And
then, more expansively, 'He said you were unusually
good and that if you worked hard he would very
much like to hear you again in a year's time and see
what might be done with you.'

'He meant—*he* might do something with me?'
Amanda caught her breath.

'Yes.' Lewis Elsworth smiled not unkindly. 'That
was what he meant. So you see why I don't want
any Max Arrowsmith pushing on to the scene.'

'Oh—' she made an impatient little brushing-off
movement with her hand—'you can dismiss him from
your mind. No mention has been made of him and
I'm sure none will be.'

She was on the point of adding that Jerome Leydon, far from misdirecting her career, actually intended to take her to hear the Warrenders. But
before she could do so Lewis Elsworth pushed up
his glasses on to his forehead in that gesture which
she now knew indicated that he was slightly nervous
and said,

'I'm very pleased with the impression you made
on Warrender, Amanda. I know I'm sparing with
expressions of approval. But you sang magnificently
on Wednesday and I was proud of you—and the
work we've done together. I thought perhaps you
might like some sort of celebration—you've certainly earned it. I have two tickets for the Warrender
concert tomorrow and I'd like to take you.'

He was smiling—really smiling full at her in that
moment, so that her dismay was all the more intense. And, after the first second, all the more ob-

vious. The smile stiffened and faded, his expression became wooden and withdrawn and he said quickly, 'Oh—you can't get away, you mean?'

'Not—not really.' Amanda snatched at something less than the unacceptable truth. 'It's such very short notice, you see, and—and——'

'I know. The usual trouble. You can't get away from the hotel.'

Amanda made a slight movement of her head which might have been interpreted as a nod. For, though she did not want to commit herself to a genuine lie—particularly when Nan had been so good about letting her go—still less did she want to admit to her teacher that she was going to that self-same concert with Jerome Leydon.

'It doesn't matter.' His studiedly casual tone did not conceal the fact that somehow it did matter very much indeed. 'It was just an idea. I'll let someone else have the tickets. There may be another chance some other time.'

'I do hope so!' Amanda spoke with genuine fervour, suddenly realising how very much she would have liked to go to that concert in his company. The company of someone who could explain and share with her a wonderful experience.

He immediately turned to the business of the lesson after that and, during the rest of the evening, there was no further opportunity for them to discuss anything even remotely personal.

She told herself that she had got out of that awkward situation pretty well on the whole. But what lingered uncomfortably with her afterwards—even when she was in bed that night—was the way his bright look of pleasure had stiffened into embarrassed disappointment when he realised that his invitation was about to be refused.

The next afternoon, with the fairly good-tempered co-operation of Nan, Amanda left in good time to catch her train to London, and all the way to town she felt a tide of excited anticipation rising within her. Any unwelcome thoughts of Lewis Elsworth, or what he had said about Jerome Leydon, faded into the back of her mind, and she thought only of the pleasure of dining with a charming and distinguished companion and sharing with him afterwards what promised to be a magnificent concert.

He was waiting at the barrier for her, looking handsome, vivid and interesting. The sort of man people glanced at twice, as though they might have seen him before or would expect to see him again in unusual circumstances.

'It's that subtle aura of success,' thought Amanda with a sudden flash of insight as he greeted her. And when he lightly took her arm as they walked across to the Festival Hall together, she was aware of a feeling of pleasure and well-being—even a touch of innocent pride—to be walking with such an interesting companion.

When they entered the restaurant, with its long stretch of windows looking out across the river to the mellow pile of Somerset House, she saw that he was greeted as someone of importance with the kind of smiles usually reserved for honoured patrons. It was all rather heady and enjoyable, and she was pleased to see that they were being escorted to one of the coveted window tables.

Then she thought there must have been some mistake, for there was someone already sitting there. A man considerably older than Jerome Leydon, with an air of owning, if not the Festival Hall, at

least a good part of whatever made up his particular
world.

He stood up as they reached the table and, as she
hesitated, Jerome said, just behind her, 'I want you
to meet my friend Max Arrowsmith, Amanda. This
is the girl I was telling you about, Max. And if you
want more than my word for the fact that she has
a very unusual talent, let me tell you that none other
than Oscar Warrender thinks well of her.'

CHAPTER THREE

AMANDA was so taken aback by the sudden introduction to Max Arrowsmith that she would literally
have retreated a step if Jerome Leydon's friendly
arm had not propelled her forward; and she found
herself taking the outstretched hand offered to her
while she murmured some conventional reply.

The voice in which Jerome's friend greeted her
was unusually deep, with very slight guttural over-
tones, and the shrewd, heavily lidded eyes which
momentarily surveyed her gave Amanda the strange
impression that their owner had looked on most
things and found them pretty poor stuff.

He was very agreeable to her, however, and was
obviously on good terms with her companion.
Neither of them embarrassed her by any further
reference to her talents, and by the time the meal
had been ordered and a few trivial remarks exchanged she felt her sense of shock lessen. If Lewis
Elsworth had not happened to speak about the con-
nection between these two she would have found
nothing strange in the encounter, she told herself.
And presently she felt almost—though not quite—at
ease.

Then the older man turned to her and remarked,
'You're going to hear the Warrenders for the first
time, I understand?'

'Yes.' Amanda smiled at him. 'I'm excited about
it.'

'Well, he's that rare thing—a genius,' Max Arrowsmith conceded, without qualification, which made Amanda feel better disposed towards him. 'And she's a very fine singer indeed, which should interest you since you're a singer yourself.'

'Oh, I'm not a singer!' Amanda assured him earnestly. 'I'm a singing student, which is quite a different thing.'

'She's too modest,' Jerome interjected with a laugh, but the other man raised his hand and said,

'Let her speak for herself. How advanced a student are you, Miss Amanda?'

'Well, Sir Oscar said I needed another year's study before—before he might be interested in me.'

'Sir Oscar's standards are high, aren't they? And he was thinking in terms of operatic singing, I take it?'

'I—I imagine so,' Amanda agreed.

'Is that your ultimate ambition?' he enquired. And then, as she did not answer immediately, he went on thoughtfully, 'You never considered a less ambitious start? Something which might give you a certain amount of stage experience without making tremendous demands on your singing development?'

Amanda shook her head, aware of an obscure sense of excitement mingled with a vague feeling of unease.

'What have you done so far?' he asked in a friendly tone, and again he silenced Jerome, who made a movement to join in the conversation at that point.

'I—I'm in a very good church choir, and have an opportunity to do some solo singing from time to time. And I have regular lessons with the choir-master, who's exceptionally good,' Amanda told him. But even to her own ears, and before Max Arrowsmith made a disparaging little grimace, that sounded rather small beer.

'And that's all?'

Amanda nodded. But this time Jerome refused to be silenced and exclaimed, 'I think someone should explain that though the man who has been teaching her is academically very good, he's one of those super-careful organists who would hardly look beyond the church door. The limit of his ambitions for her would probably be "Hear ye, Israel" or something of the sort.'

A faint resentment rose in Amanda at this cavalier dismissal of her success on the previous Wednesday, and she felt she almost liked Max Arrowsmith when he observed drily, '"Hear ye, Israel" takes a lot of singing.'

'Of course it does,' Jerome Leydon agreed impatiently. 'And Amanda has demonstrated that it's almost child's play to her. That's why I maintain that she could sing almost anything we might be interested in. And, as you see, she's pretty and has a certain style and——'

'She's very pretty,' agreed the older man, and he smiled at Amanda indulgently, so that she wondered why she had thought him slightly dangerous at first. 'And she has, as you say, got style. We must think about her.'

'In—in what way, Mr Arrowsmith?' asked Amanda timidly.

'Well, this isn't quite the moment—or the place—to go into details.' He glanced at his watch. 'It's getting near concert time. But I should like to hear you sing one of these days.'

Then he raised his hand peremptorily to the

waiter, and Amanda was both relieved and disappointed to realise that this disturbing but intriguing conversation was over. They all three left the
restaurant together, but she found that Max Arrowsmith was not accompanying them to the concert.
He bade them goodnight at the foot of the stairs and
she thought it was not just an empty courtesy when
he said he hoped he would see her again quite soon.

'I hope so too,' she replied, not entirely sincerely, and turned away quickly in slight embarrassment. As she did so she knocked against someone's
arm, glanced up to apologise and found herself
looking into the surprised and angry eyes of Lewis
Elsworth.

'Why—why, hello,' she heard herself say rather
idiotically. And he replied, 'Hello,' very coldly and
passed on.

It was one of the most horrible moments she had
ever experienced, and she found herself thinking—
if *only* she had told him the truth when she had to
refuse his invitation! Or, alternatively, if only Max
Arrowsmith had left them five minutes earlier! At
least she would then have had to do no more than
explain, as best she could, the fact that she was with
Jerome. Now, with the wretched tangle of circumstances, it must seem to him that she had deliberately
deceived him, not only with regard to Jerome Leydon, but Max Arrowsmith too.

Trembling with chagrin and dismay, she turned
back to Jerome, whose attention had been caught by
another acquaintance, and she realised thankfully
that he had not seen her encounter with Lewis Elsworth. It was not much to be thankful for in a horrid
and humiliating situation, but at least it was something. All the same, it seemed to her now that she

could not possibly enjoy any concert. But, once she
was seated in the hall and aware of the expectant
hush, succeeded by the outburst of applause which
greeted the conductor's entrance, she somehow
sensed that this was going to be one of those rare
occasions when all personal worries must give way
to a tremendous overall experience.

She was not sufficiently knowledgeable to judge
just why this concert was different from anything
else she had ever heard. It was simply that nothing
seemed to stand between her and the music; rather
as though the work were flowing straight from the
mind and heart of the composer for the first time
and she, Amanda Lovett, were the incredibly fortunate creature for whom it had been composed. It
did not occur to her that this was the impression
made on almost everyone else in the hall, until she
was startled by the applause at the end and the
realisation that this held a quality of astonishment
and something like gratitude in it.

'Well?' said Jerome Leydon beside her, and she
turned her head to see that he was smiling indulgently, as though enjoying her enjoyment.

'Nothing,' replied Amanda. 'There's simply nothing to add, is there? It's all been said, and I can't
think that Mozart would have wanted it any
different.'

'Right first time,' Jerome told her with a laugh,
and he patted her hand approvingly and then left his
hand on hers.

She stared down at their two hands for a moment,
half moved by his approval, half thrilled by the
warmth of his clasp. Then Warrender led on Anthea
and, returning to the rostrum, took his orchestra

through the opening bars of the Letter Scene from *Eugene Onegin*.

By now, of course, Amanda knew a good deal more about the mechanics of singing than of conducting, and she could appreciate to the full the beauty of Anthea's performance. Not only the consummate singing, but the drama which she infused into the scene while still keeping, with perfect taste, within the confines of the concert platform.

'She's lovely!' Amanda turned delightedly to her companion. 'If I ever sing half as well as that I'll be proud and happy.'

'You'll go further than halfway,' he assured her. 'Not necessarily on exactly the same path, but I don't mind prophesying, Amanda, that you have a real future in front of you.'

She was happy, of course, to hear him say that. But the reference to a different path brought back some of her earlier disquiet during the scene with Max Arrowsmith and then—much worse—her anguish over the encounter with Lewis Elsworth. So that, although she greatly enjoyed the rest of the concert, at the edge of her pleasure was the small, niggling distress about her singing teacher. She tried to tell herself that his disapproval need not matter *so* much. But what really made her wretched was the thought that she must seem despicable in his eyes.

Even when she was going backstage with Jerome Leydon later, the fear that she might meet Lewis Elsworth transcended any pleasure in the new experience. But they were delayed several times by people who wanted to speak to Jerome and, by the time they arrived in the Warrenders' dressing-room, the crowds had thinned and she was able to see that, if Lewis Elsworth had indeed come, he had now already gone.

Immensely relieved, she was able to voice her eager enthusiasm to Anthea Warrender, who said quite sincerely, 'Thank you. But the conducting has a lot to do with it, you know. You'll find out for yourself one of these days that for a singer a good conductor is half the battle.'

'Don't take that as a totally unprejudiced opinion,' said Warrender with a dry smile, and Amanda found the courage to ask,

'Sir Oscar, how was it that the music all sounded so incredibly *new*—as though it had just happened? I mean—you must have conducted each one of those works many times.'

'Thank you for that compliment—the most subtle you can pay any conductor,' Warrender said to her, with a sudden and very brilliant smile. 'And I'll tell you the simple answer. One should always remember that someone, somewhere in the audience, is hearing even, let's say, Schubert's "Unfinished" for the first time—and for that one person the conductor should conduct.' Then he added, almost in an undertone and as though to himself, 'Think of the *wonder* of hearing Schubert's "Unfinished" for the first time!'

Anthea laughed and patted his arm affectionately before turning away to ask Jerome something, and for a moment Amanda found herself alone with the conductor. And suddenly, on an impulse she could never afterwards explain, she said breathlessly, 'Sir Oscar, may I ask you something?'

'If you feel you must,' was the not altogether encouraging reply.

'Do you—do you know someone called Max Arrowsmith?'

'Certainly I know Max Arrowsmith. Why?'

'What do you think of him?' Amanda asked earnestly.

'What do I *think* of him? As a businessman, do you mean?—or a person?'

'Well, both, I suppose.'

'As a businessman he's immensely clever. Probably one of the toughest eggs ever hatched. As a person——?' the conductor gave that some further consideration. 'Well, Miss—Amanda, isn't it?' Amanda nodded silently. 'There was a description coined long ago for someone else, but I think it could be applied fairly to Max Arrowsmith. He knows the price of everything and the value of nothing. Now run along. It's getting late.'

Amanda rejoined Jerome at once and presently, their goodbyes completed, she found herself outside the Hall with him, walking towards the car park.

'Well?' He took her arm in that friendly, almost intimate way. 'How was the whole experience?'

'It was the first really great conducting I've ever heard,' she said, slightly pressing his hand against her without even realising what she was doing. 'And Anthea Warrender is, of course, the loveliest singer in my experience. In fact, it was a magical evening from be——' she stopped.

'From beginning to end?' he finished for her. 'Or did you, on reflection, decide that some of it was not quite up to expectation?'

'Oh, no! Nothing like that at all. In fact, I can't possibly thank you enough for your kindness and generosity. It's just that—I was a little disturbed by one or two things Mr Arrowsmith said.'

'You need not be,' he told her lightly. 'He looks a little bit the stage villain, I grant you. But he's a very good fellow really.'

She wanted to say that was not quite the way Sir Oscar Warrender had described him. But tact towards her host, and caution for she knew not what, silenced her and she let the subject of Max Arrowsmith drop.

The drive home was rapid, pleasant and uneventful. She was suddenly tired after all the varied experiences of the evening and Jerome seemed to sense that, leaving her for a good part of the way to easy and strangely companionable silence. Only when the countryside was beginning to look familiar and Amanda realised they were not very far from home, he said,

'I've told Diana—my sister, you know—quite a bit about you, and she's keen to meet you. She'll probably drop in at The Nightingale one of these days, just to say hello. All right with you and your people?'

'Why, of course!' Amanda roused herself to express genuine pleasure, both for the friendly overture from someone she did not want to lose sight of and also for the thought that the contact would be pleasant and even helpful to Nan. 'My brother and sister-in-law will be delighted. They're both sociable people, and Nan at any rate is greatly interested in music. She once had hopes herself of being a singer, but when my brother was badly injured motor-racing——'

'Your brother isn't *Henry* Lovett, the racing driver, is he?' interrupted Jerome.

'Yes!' She turned in her seat to smile at him with pleasure. 'Do you remember him?'

'But of course. He was a hero of mine when I was about sixteen. I even asked him for his autograph once.' Jerome grinned reminiscently.

'Oh, you *didn't*!'

'Certainly I did. Why not? Most of my age-group thought the world of him. He was so young himself then—not more than twenty, I imagine. He seemed almost like one of us, and yet he did all the godlike things we longed to do.'

'Oh, Jerome, how nice of you to speak of him like that!' She laughed, though she was oddly moved too. 'I'll tell him. Or better still, come and meet him yourself some time. It would mean a lot to him. He doesn't get much chance these days to talk of his racing years.'

'That's a promise,' Jerome told her with obvious satisfaction. 'I suppose that accident put paid to most things for him?'

'I'm afraid it did. He made a better recovery than anyone dared to hope at the time, but there were some very difficult years. Then he and my sister-in-law took over The Nightingale and, though it's been a tough struggle, they're beginning to break even, and rather more than that now.'

'I'm glad,' he said sincerely, as they drove up to the silent house where the sign of The Nightingale swung gently to and fro in the night wind. 'And I'm glad to know that we shall be seeing something of each other in the future, Amanda.'

'Yes, indeed!' All her gratitude for a wonderful evening went into that, and it seemed very fitting that he should lean forward and kiss her lightly as he helped her out of the car. It was not a demanding kiss. Just a friendly, almost casual one; and as such it was acceptable.

He waited while she let herself in at a side door and then, with a final wave to her, he got back into his car and drove off. Amanda was glad the place remained silent as she closed the door. It was reassuring to know that no one else was up and that she would not therefore have to give any account of her evening until she had had time to consider every detail herself. But, in point of fact, hardly had she got into bed than she was asleep. And it seemed to be no more than a matter of minutes before the light was pouring into her room.

There was very little time to prepare whatever she was going to say, but she made of it all an entertaining story which amused and rather charmed both her brother and Nan. She even included Max Arrowsmith in her account, at which Nan wrinkled her forehead thoughtfully and said, 'He's some sort of impresario, isn't he?'

'Yes,' said Amanda, helping herself to toast. 'Sir Oscar says he's pretty tough but a very clever businessman.—And I found that Jerome Leydon is a fan of yours, Henry.' And she added a résumé of the last conversation in the car on the way home.

As she expected, her brother was both amused and pleased, and even Nan smiled indulgently and said she would like it if Jerome and his sister did drop in.

The only thing Amanda left out of her story was the encounter with Lewis Elsworth. And yet, illogically enough, the feeling began to grow upon her that this was the most important thing which had happened during the evening and, as a natural corollary, that she must do something about it. She had no special plan of action. She only knew that she must see Lewis Elsworth. And, with some ingenuity, she concocted a fairly good reason for going over to Austin Parva that afternoon.

'Won't it wait until tomorrow?' Nan wanted to know. 'You'll be going there then anyway for your choir practice.'

Tense with nervousness at the very thought of delay, Amanda managed to say consideringly that she thought it better to go that afternoon and, Nan making no further objection, she set off on her bicycle as soon as the lunchtime rush was over.

Since all her lessons were conducted in the church schoolroom, and the choir practices of course in the church, she had hardly ever had any occasion to call at the small, white-painted house at the end of the main village street, and only twice had she even stepped inside the door. Her hand was not entirely steady as she pulled at the brightly polished brass knob which rang a bell somewhere in the back regions of the house, and she was aware suddenly that her breath was coming unevenly as she heard footsteps approaching the door.

It was he himself who opened the door—as she had expected since she knew he lived alone—and he looked startled and not at all pleased when he saw who was standing there.

'May I come in, please?' said Amanda without preamble. 'I—I want to speak to you.'

He pulled the door further open then and stood aside for her to enter.

'Go through to the room at the back,' he said. 'At least——'

But she gave him no opportunity to develop any alternative plan, and went through the small house and into an unusually beautiful room, with panelled walls and ceiling and a wide view of an unexpectedly large and colourful garden. Near the wide windows stood a full-sized concert grand piano, and on the large polished mahogany table sheets of manuscript music were scattered.

As he followed her into the room he went over to the table and swept the sheets of manuscript together, pushing them half out of sight. Almost, thought Amanda, as though he did not want her to see them.

He did not ask her to sit down, so she stood, and the only thing she could think of to say was the sentence which had been repeating itself in her head all the way there.

'I want to explain about last night.' It came out as a plain, unvarnished, rather aggressive statement.

'Is there anything to explain?'

'Yes, of course there is! You must have thought me both rude and deceitful, but——'

'I did,' he agreed, and that also came out as a plain, unvarnished, rather aggressive statement, which made her wince.

'I can't blame you. But it wasn't quite as—as it sounds. Before you invited me to go to the Warrender concert with you. Jerome Leydon had already invited me and I'd accepted. I was sorry and—and embarrassed when I had to refuse you——'

'Why?'

'*Why?*' she repeated, realising suddenly that she had not even thought about that until this moment. She sat down slowly—though still uninvited—and leant her arms on the big polished table. 'I think,' she said, trying to reconstruct the scene in her mind and seeing it with unexpected clarity, 'I think mostly because you gave your invitation with such real pleasure; you smiled as though it made you happy to be offering me the very nicest treat you could think of, and I *hated* knowing I must refuse. You evidently saw what was coming because the—the light went out of your face and——'

'I had no idea that I had such a speaking countenance,' he said drily, but he too sat down at the table then, facing her.

'You don't usually,' she told him. 'That's what made it all the more—distressing.'

'You're too easily distressed,' he told her coldly.

'Anyway,' she rushed on quickly, 'when I knew I had to refuse I didn't want to add insult to injury by admitting I was already going to the concert with someone you—you apparently don't much like. So I let you think it was just a matter of my not being able to get away from the hotel. It was a spur-of-the-moment decision, and I realise now it was a stupid one. I'm sorry. I probably deserved being shown up later, but——'

'And how does Max Arrowsmith—of whom you'd never heard—come into this?' he enquired, again in that dry tone.

'Oh, he was just a sort of bonus to the malignant fate who seems to have mixed all the lines for me!' She gave a rather desperate little laugh which, to her horror, sounded extraordinarily unsteady. 'I truly *had* never met him or even heard of him. He joined us at dinner. There was nothing I could do about it, even if—if——' the unsteadiness in her voice increased and she struggled to find her handkerchief, but, failing to do so, wiped the back of her hand across her eyes instead.

'Please don't start crying. It makes me nervous,' he said, though she could not detect the slightest sign of nervousness in his manner. Then he handed her a handkerchief across the table and, when she had clumsily wiped her eyes, he said, 'Go on.'

'I *can't* go on. Not when you talk like that. And anyway, there's nothing else to say. Except once more that I'm sorry and—and I think I'd better go now. Perhaps I'd have done better not to have come anyway,' she added and, a good deal ashamed of the scene she had made, she got to her feet.

'Sit down, Amanda, and stop being a silly little idiot,' Lewis said bracingly. 'You're making too much of this whole affair. I accept your explanation, though I still deplore the Leydon–Arrowsmith combination. Now would you like a cup of tea? It's the recognised remedy for an emotional upset, isn't it?'

He smiled straight at her then, in a way she found amazingly reassuring, so that she found herself able to smile back at him, though a little uncertainly.

'Th-thank you. That would be nice,' she admitted, and a great wave of relief engulfed her as she realised that his 'I accept your explanation' meant far more than she could ever have supposed possible. 'Can I come and help you?' she offered.

'No, stay where you are. I won't be five minutes.'

So she stayed where she was, sitting at the table, experiencing some feeling not unlike that wonderful moment when the convalescent realises that recovery is imminent after all. She glanced out at the riot of colour in the garden and then back at the pile of music manuscript on the table, then she leaned forward and drawing the top sheet towards her began to examine it with some curiosity.

It was nothing she recognised, although it was obviously a song of some kind, and she instinctively began to sight-read it, humming it under her breath.

She was still absorbed in the manuscript sheet when Lewis came back into the room, carrying a tray, and she looked up and said, 'What are you copying here? It's nothing I know, but it's rather lovely, isn't it?'

'Is it?' He set down the tray with some deliberation, as though he were absorbed in keeping everything steady. 'I wouldn't know.'

'But what is it? And who wrote it?'

'I did,' he replied after a fractional pause.

'*You* did? But I had no idea you composed!'

'Well, there's no special reason why you should, is there? Milk and sugar?'

'Yes, please,' she said absently, and returned her attention to the sheet in her hand. 'I love that unusual rising interval in the opening phrase.' She sang it in full voice and then got up suddenly and went to the piano. 'Come and play it for me, will you? I'd like to sing it right through.'

'Don't you want your tea?' He stood unnaturally still, watching her.

'Tea?' she repeated vaguely. 'Oh—no, thank you. I mean—not while there's something like this to sing.' She opened the keyboard of the piano and actually held out her hand to him, as though she were encouraging someone younger than herself.

He came over to her, taking the outstretched hand for a moment in an unexpectedly tight grip, then he sat down and began to play. Amanda stood behind him and sang with some confidence, though she had to lean almost over his shoulder once or twice to catch the exact word or note. He stopped her once and in a slightly husky voice directed her back to the beginning of a line, and she followed with meticulous care what he had told her.

At the end she continued to stand behind him, silent now and moved in some indescribable way to a degree she had never experienced before. He too was silent, as he took off his glasses and reached vaguely into his pocket for his handkerchief.

'It's here. You lent it to me—remember?' And, picking up the handkerchief, she handed it to him. He took it without thanks and slowly polished his glasses. Then he said,

'It sounds different when you sing it.'

'You mean I didn't do it quite the way you intended?'

'No. I mean that though notes can tell you a lot in a—an academic way, it's a different thing when someone sings them—very beautifully. I didn't know—' he cleared his throat slightly—'that it was quite a good song.'

'It's a lovely song,' she said. And then, lest the moment should become too emotional, she went to take her cup of tea from the tray and, seeing the other cup was empty, she filled it for him and brought it back to him as he still sat at the piano.

'Thank you.' He took it absently, as though it were quite natural for her to wait on him in his own home.

'Have you composed anything else like that?' she asked him presently.

'Not any other vocal music—no.' He shook his head. 'I've done things for the organ and some string music. I composed a string quartet early in the year and sent it in for a music contest. Warrender was one of the judges. When he came down here the other evening——'

'Oh, *that's* why you spoke as though he might be in Austin Parva for something other than my singing?'

'It did occur to me. But only for a moment. Then

after the choir practice he talked to me for some time and said that, in his view, whatever talent I had was almost certainly for vocal music——'

'Did he say it was a very considerable talent?' she interrupted quickly.

'Well, yes, he did. And he made the suggestion that I should try my hand at a simple song.' He paused and gave an odd, almost shy little smile. 'That's the song.' He gestured towards the sheet of manuscript music on the piano.

'But, Lewis——' suddenly that was the perfectly natural way to address him—'it's absolutely lovely! You're a genius!'

'Oh, no, I'm not!' He laughed then in his usual forthright, unsentimental way. 'This may be just a flash in the pan.'

'You know it isn't!' she said indignantly.

'All right, I know it isn't,' he agreed quite seriously. 'But one song doesn't make a composer. This could be the beginning of something—or not. I just don't know yet.'

'Where did you get the words?' Amanda asked interestedly.

'From a mixed collection of short poems which I found in a secondhand bookshop,' he admitted. 'It's one of those nineteenth-century things which hover somewhere between pure gold and pure corn. The music can make all the difference,' he added. 'And so can the way it's sung.' He smiled at her. 'Thank you, Amanda. You've given me something this afternoon which has more than paid for all your lessons.'

'Oh! What a lovely thing to say. Particularly after the ridiculous way I behaved over the concert. Thank *you*, Lewis, for all you've done for me. I'm going to make a prophecy. I think you'll write an opera one day. Perhaps a chamber opera,' she added hastily, as he made a quick gesture of repudiating such an idea.

'All right. And perhaps you'll sing in it,' he retorted lightly, as he accompanied her to the door and watched her remount her bicycle. 'Go carefully.'

And she had reached the far end of the village street, and was just passing the church, before it occurred to her that never before had he said anything which expressed the least concern for her personal welfare.

With a strong wind behind her and her spirits and energy at their highest, she made good time on the way home and, as she entered The Nightingale, she was aware of the sound of several voices coming from the family sitting room, with a certain amount of laughter and the general impression of gay conversation.

The tones of her brother and sister-in-law were easily distinguishable, but with them was another voice which sounded excitingly familiar. And when she entered the room she was not surprised—but exceedingly pleased—to find Jerome Leydon there. With him was a good-looking woman slightly older than he was, but sufficiently like him to suggest that she must be his sister, Diana.

Both of them were in animated conversation with Nan and Henry. The other person in the room, who was not joining in the conversation at the moment, she recognised with a slight sense of shock as Max Arrowsmith.

'Here she is!' cried Nan, on a note of unforced gaiety which Amanda had not heard from her for a long time. 'Mandy, come and meet Mr Leydon's sister, Mrs Cole. You know everyone else, I think. Even—you secretive creature—Mr Arrowsmith.'

'I wasn't secretive about Mr Arrowsmith,' Amanda protested, as she shook hands in turn with the three visitors. 'I told you about meeting him.'

'But you didn't tell us about his special interest in you. How *could* you keep quiet about your voice and your lessons with Dr Elsworth—and Sir Oscar thinking well of you? And perhaps most of all Mr Arrowsmith's interest.'

'I didn't know Mr Arrowsmith was specially interested in me,' said Amanda stubbornly, while she felt as though a great gusty wind was beginning to blow upon her future.

'But he *says* he is,' reiterated Nan. 'That's right, isn't it, Mr Arrowsmith?'

'Yes, that's right,' agreed Max Arrowsmith. And again those dark, heavily-lidded eyes regarded Amanda a little inscrutably.

CHAPTER FOUR

RELIEVED though she was to find that Henry—and, still more importantly, Nan—had calmly accepted the revelation about her singing, Amanda was disquieted by the presence of Mr Arrowsmith. Little more than an hour ago Lewis Elsworth had been expressing strong disapproval of him, and now here he was, seemingly entrenched in the family circle on quite friendly terms.

Somehow she summoned a nervous smile of general greeting, and then addressed herself to her sister-in-law.

'Nan, I'm so glad you and Henry know about—everything at last,' she said eagerly. 'I hated not telling you before this. But, knowing what I did of your own talent and frustrated career, how *could* I start babbling about my modest hopes? After all, they may come to nothing and——'

'I wouldn't be too sure of their coming to nothing,' put in Max Arrowsmith. 'Not,' he added carelessly, 'if you have good advice—and follow it.'

'There you are!' Nan's eyes sparkled with such pleasure that Amanda felt strangely moved. Who could have supposed that Nan, of all people, would rejoice so openly on her behalf?

In an attempt to avoid a tricky subject, she turned away then to accept Jerome's introduction to his sister. And Diana Cole smiled at her with obvious interest and said, 'Congratulations! This is really very exciting, isn't it?'

'Oh, it's too early for congratulations,' Amanda protested quickly. 'Dr Elsworth thinks——'

'Don't rely solely on his advice, Amanda,' interrupted Jerome with good-humoured firmness. 'He's a splendid basic teacher, of course. But though I'm not knocking him, the fact is that a village organist is hardly the best person to advise about a stage career.'

'I'm not ready for any sort of stage career yet,' retorted Amanda, her annoyance on Lewis's behalf adding emphasis to that.

'That could be a matter of opinion,' observed Max Arrowsmith. And because he sounded rather amused Amanda said quite rudely,

'Whose opinion?'

'Eventually—mine, when I've heard you and had an opportunity to make my own assessment,' was the cool reply. 'Meanwhile I'm impressed by what Jerome has told me, and neither he nor I could be described as inexperienced in these matters.'

'You do realise Mr Arrowsmith's position in the theatre world, Mandy, don't you?' Nan interjected eagerly. 'And Mr Leydon is a composer who——'

'Lewis Elsworth is also a composer,' Amanda heard herself state rather aggressively. And then she immediately wondered if she had betrayed a confidence. Certainly her statement produced a pregnant silence, which was broken after a moment by Jerome saying curiously,

'So he composes, does he? What does he compose?—Church anthems?'

She very much wanted to say that Oscar Warrender was interested in Jerome's compositions; but she was afraid she might already have said too much to an audience less than friendly towards her teacher.

So she choked back her indignant defence and replied not quite truthfully, 'I don't know any details. I haven't discussed it with him.'

Then, suddenly aware that she was disturbing the harmony of the scene unnecessarily, she smiled and said apologetically, 'Don't think I'm ungrateful for all this interest in my voice. It's just—I'm rather bemused with the suddenness of it all. And, as I said before, these are early days. Too early for me to make any firm plans.'

Nan made as though to speak and so did Jerome, but it was characteristically Mr Arrowsmith who got in the first word.

'Miss Lovett,' he said, 'your loyalty to your teacher does you credit, and if he has taught you as well as Jerome says then you're right to display it. But behind every successful artist you'll usually find more than one adviser, one teacher, one director of talent. From my own observation and from what Jerome has told me, I think you're probably quite ready to be tested for something other than operatic singing; something which would give you some professional stage experience and stand you in good stead in any future ambitions.'

'What—exactly—did you have in mind?' Amanda was half reassured against her will.

'My dear—' Max Arrowsmith got to his feet with a smile, but with an air of putting an end to the conversation—'in show business no one puts all his cards on the table at the first discussion. Least of all myself. I suggest that Jerome brings you to London some time during the next few days and that I have a chance of hearing and testing you for myself. You may, of course, prove to be no good at all.' He made a disparaging little gesture which, curiously enough, had the effect of putting Amanda on her mettle. 'But I should like to judge for myself,' he concluded.

Then, without waiting for any reply from her, he turned to Nan, who was listening with breathless interest, and said, 'Mrs Lovett, it has been a charming—possibly a fruitful—visit and I hope we shall all be seeing more of each other.'

As goodbyes were exchanged Jerome gave Amanda's hand a specially friendly pressure and whispered, 'Trust me! I'll see everything goes all right for you.'

The three visitors then departed and Nan, having watched them from the window as they got into their car, turned and exclaimed, 'You lucky, lucky girl! You say so little. I suppose you're just stunned by your good fortune.'

But before she could answer, Henry asked curiously, 'What have you against Arrowsmith, Mandy?' and she turned to him almost gratefully.

'Nothing specific, I suppose,' she conceded. 'But——'

'I should think not indeed!' Nan's quick laugh was scornful. 'This could be a chance in a million for you.'

'It could,' Amanda admitted. 'But what I was going to say was that we don't know much about Mr Arrowsmith, except that he's obviously very successful and used to getting his own way regardless of other people. To the best of my knowledge he's largely concerned with a side of the musical world which is less serious, less—' she groped for the right word—'oh, less worthwhile, I suppose, than the kind of thing Dr Elsworth has in mind for me.'

'You seem completely under that man's influence,'

Nan exclaimed discontentedly. 'No doubt he means well but, as Jerome said, he's only a village choirmaster when all's said and done.'

'Some of the best singers have been grateful to have started under the guidance of a village choirmaster,' retorted Amanda angrily. 'And I don't know what you mean by *only*. He's a very fine musician and organist, a quite marvellous vocal teacher and—and a composer in his own right.'

'All of which need not rule out the thrilling fact that Max Arrowsmith—one of the most influential men in the theatre world—is sufficiently interested to want to hear you and perhaps take a hand in your career. What's the objection?'

'I don't think Dr Elsworth has a very high opinion of him,' Amanda said unwillingly.

'Oh, Elsworth—Elsworth! You seem quite infatuated with the man. What's his special magic, for goodness' sake?'

'I'm *not* infatuated!' The word stung Amanda with quite unexpected sharpness. 'What a ridiculous word to use! I owe him a lot. I like him as a person, and I have great faith in his judgment. Naturally I quote his opinions.'

'Fine,' said Nan, but she gave her young sister-in-law a rather thoughtful glance, before taking herself off to the kitchen with the observation that business must go on.

Amanda and her brother exchanged a rather rueful smile, and he said, 'She's taken it very well, considering how cruelly she was cheated of her own career.'

'Oh, I know—I know!' Amanda was immediately remorseful. 'I think I'm over-excited and—and a little scared and not behaving very sensibly.' Then she added curiously, 'What did *you* think of Mr Arrowsmith, Henry?'

'On such a short acquaintance?' Her brother laughed rather protestingly. 'I suppose he could do a great deal for you, Mandy, if you liked to remain on the right side of him. You're a bit too young and inexperienced to be dogmatic to an old stager like that. It's fine to have high ambitions, but unwise, I should have thought, to reject any sort of influential support at such an early stage.'

'You're right, of course.' Amanda drew a quick breath of relief as her brother's dictum seemed to absolve her from making any immediate decision.

'I suppose these show business people tend to blow hot and cold,' Henry added slowly. 'Why don't you keep all talk of this conversation to yourself until something concrete comes up?'

'Not tell Dr Elsworth, you mean? Wouldn't that be rather—underhand?'

'Depends on your relationship,' replied her brother. 'Are you in the habit of telling him everything?—You're not?'—as Amanda shook her head. 'Then why tell him this before there's anything much to tell? He can't form an opinion—or shouldn't presume to form an opinion—before you know just what Arrowsmith's offer involves. If nothing comes of it you'll just look silly, and if something does come of it there'll be a basis for discussion. Not before.'

This appealed so much to Amanda that she felt her nervous tension begin to relax, and for the rest of that evening she was her usual cheerful self. She thought Henry must have spoken to Nan on much the same lines. At any rate her sister-in-law said little more about their visitors, except that it had been fun to see some interesting company for once.

The next day Amanda went to her lesson as usual, but on the way there had some qualms about her decision to say nothing about the visit of Mr Arrowsmith and Jerome. She need not have worried. Lewis was very much the absorbed singing master, intent on nothing but the task of extracting the best work possible from his student. If anything, he was even more than usually reserved and impersonal, so that she wondered if he were regretting the very different relationship which had been briefly established the previous afternoon and was deliberately re-creating the more formal atmosphere of master and student.

At any other time she might have been disappointed. As it was, she was relieved not to have to discuss anything but her lesson and the subsequent choir practice.

During the next few days she hovered illogically between relief over the absence of drama and disappointment that nothing was happening. Then on Saturday evening Jerome telephoned, his voice vibrant with friendly interest. And what he said was, 'It's all arranged, Amanda.'

'What's all arranged?' she asked, feeling her heart excitedly skip a beat and then begin to thump anxiously.

'Stop playing hard to get,' he told her with a laugh. 'I've arranged for Arrowsmith to hear you and discuss possibilities with you, and I'm driving you up to town myself and holding a watching brief for my favourite soprano. Now don't start raising objections. You're talking to a very determined man.'

'I'm not going to raise objections.' She too laughed, but a little breathlessly. 'And I'm more than grateful to you, Jerome.'

'My real friends call me Jerry,'

'Jerry, then. When is the appointment?'

'Wednesday next. I'll collect you about two-thirty.'

'I can't come on Wednesday,' she exclaimed quickly. 'I have my singing lesson then—and choir practice.'

There was a slight pause. Then Jerome said, 'I'm holding my breath and counting ten, Amanda Lovett. You do realise that most singing students would give their back teeth for a chance to sing to Max Arrowsmith, don't you?'

'Yes, yes, I do. And I'm terribly sorry. But does it *have* to be Wednesday? I mean, it's so difficult to make an excuse or explain or——'

'Dear,' said Jerome in a tone of barely controlled impatience, 'it does have to be Wednesday, because Arrowsmith is a busy and influential man who makes appointments to suit himself. It's the other people who keep them. Tell Elsworth whatever you like. Tell him the truth,' he added carelessly. 'Why not?'

Why not, indeed? Except that she felt virtually sure he would be totally opposed to the idea and let her know it in no uncertain terms.

'Would you like me to make up a few acceptable excuses for you?' enquired Jerome's laughing voice at that moment. 'I'm quite good at that sort of thing.'

'No! No, thank you.' Her reaction was instantaneous, for his amused, casual offer made her see at once that it would be contemptible to fob off someone as important to her as Lewis with any old lie concocted by someone else. He was entitled to have the truth, even if this premature disclosure of her plans led to friction. 'I will be available on Wednesday, I promise. And thank you very much, Jero—Jerry. It's more than kind of you to drive me up to town.'

'Not at all. I'm not a completely disinterested party, you know. Apart from—what shall I say?—liking you enormously, I'm personally concerned in this project of Arrowsmith's.'

'In what way?' Her attention was sharply aroused.

'I'll tell you when we're on our way,' he assured her teasingly. 'Two-thirty on Wednesday. I'll collect you from The Nightingale. Wear your prettiest dress, provided you feel comfortable and relaxed in it. I want to have the real, slightly naïve Amanda much in evidence on this occasion.' And then he rang off before she could ask just what he meant by that.

Since she could not ask him to enlarge on his statement she went and looked at herself in the mirror over the mantelpiece, and tried to discover the real, slightly naïve Amanda in the reflection there. While she was doing so Nan came into the room and Amanda swung round and asked impulsively, 'Nan, would you say I look naïve?'

'*Look* naïve?' was the reply. 'You *are* naïve. But don't worry about it. There's a novel sort of charm about that quality nowadays,' she added absently, as she scribbled something down on one of her inevitable lists.

Amanda laughed, felt suddenly how really fond she was of her sister-in-law and impulsively told her, 'Nan, I'm going to London on Wednesday with Jerome Leydon. He's taking me to Max Arrowsmith to be—looked over, one might say.'

'You *are*?' Nan dropped both her list and pencil, and into her cheeks came that flush of excitement which had so touched Amanda before. 'How marvellous! Oh, Mandy, you won't take too lofty a stand, will you? One has to be practical in this very imperfect world. I'd hate it if you spoiled your chances for the sake of some highflown notions about artistic principles and that sort of thing.'

'Dear Nan—' Amanda spoke affectionately but a trifle uneasily—'how much you care about my future welfare. It's simply sweet of you when you yourself——'

'It's not sweet of me,' was the impatient reply, and Nan's voice sounded suddenly harsh. 'Don't polish a halo which simply isn't there. I do think of your good—I truly do, Mandy. But if you succeeded as Arrowsmith could make you succeed it would mean so much—so much.' She broke off suddenly and stooped to pick up her pencil and list.

'Do you mean—not only to me?' Amanda felt a slight chill which she could not explain to herself. 'Did you mean that, Nan? What is it? Is something worrying you?'

'No. Nothing at all.' Nan was her cool self again. 'Just keep your own best interests in mind, and don't offend anyone unnecessarily on Wednesday. Why——' she stopped abruptly again, and then looked directly at her young sister-in-law. 'Wednesday! It's your singing lesson—and choir practice—that day, isn't it?'

'Yes,' Amanda said.

'Do you want me to phone on the Wednesday morning and say you've got a cold or something? Or I could say we are specially busy and can't spare you. I don't mind telling a white lie for you if that would help.'

'No, thank you, Nan. It won't be necessary.' Somehow she felt deep resentment for the fact that other

people were willing to tell lies to Lewis on her behalf. 'I'll be seeing Dr Elsworth tomorrow for my
lesson before Evensong. I'll explain then.'

'You mean—tell him you're going to audition for
Arrowsmith? He's not going to like it, is he?'

'No, he's not going to like it,' Amanda said
steadily. 'But we're not on the sort of terms where I
should care to tell lies to him.' She nearly added
'again' but bit that back in time.

'Well—' Nan laughed approvingly—'I'm glad to
see you can stand up to him sometimes. I was beginning to think you attached such importance to his
slightest word that you were afraid of him.'

'Oh, no.' Amanda forced herself to smile. 'I admire and respect him, but I'm not afraid of him.'

She knew that was a lie even as she said it. And
still more did she know it was as she rode off the
following afternoon on her way to Austin Parva and
her lesson with Lewis Elsworth.

He was in a good mood that day, a much more
talkative mood than on the previous Wednesday,
and he told her almost at once that he had sent the
manuscript of his song to Oscar Warrender and had
received a highly congratulatory telephone call from
the famous conductor.

'Oh, I'm so glad!' The happy note in her voice
was primarily because of his good fortune, of course,
but also partly for the realisation that they were
starting the lesson on a most favourable footing. 'He
wants you to do more, I hope?'

'Yes, he does. He wants me to meet Kenneth Ful-
royd, the operatic composer. He's quite an old man
now and doesn't do much composing. But Warrender introduced several of his works to the public,

even though they were difficult to stage. He thinks we would have a good deal in common, as he too started as an organist and choirmaster.'

'It's a wonderful idea! and terribly exciting. As though things are really beginning to move for you.'

'Odd you should use that expression.' Lewis smiled reflectively. 'I have something the same feeling myself. Perhaps I'm a little infected by your positive optimism, Amanda. I'd like you to know that it helps. Having someone else believe in one, I mean.'

'I do believe in you—absolutely,' she said earnestly. 'In your inspiration, your judgment—oh, everything.'

'Well, temper the praise a little,' he advised her. 'I might have to reprove you during the lesson, and then what?'

But he had no reason to do so. It was as though she too were riding high on a wave of optimism. Difficulties just seemed to melt away, and at the end of the lesson he said,

'You're making big steps forward these days, Amanda. I don't often tell a student that I'm very pleased. It gives them false ideas in the early stages. But I'm more than satisfied with your progress and next week I want you to——'

She did not hear what he wanted her to do next week, for suddenly, with a horrible little shock, she dropped down off the heights to which his approval had boosted her and remembered she had to tell him about Wednesday.

'I'm so sorry, but I can't come next Wednesday,' she said. Just like that. Bluntly, without any tactful preparation or diplomatic approach.

'No?' He looked at her in surprise. 'Why not?'

'I'm going—' she swallowed—'to London.'

'Why?' That also was blunt, to the point of brutality.

'You won't be very pleased, but I prefer to tell you the truth rather than pretend this time,' she said steadily. 'When I got home the other day, to my surprise Jerome Leydon and his sister had called, and they brought Max Arrowsmith with them. He —Mr Arrowsmith—said he wanted to hear me some time, that he was interested in what Jerome Leydon had said about me.'

'You would have been wise to say then and there that you were not at the auditioning stage for anyone,' he interrupted shortly.

'I did try to say something of the kind, but no one, including my family, seemed to think that very sensible. Mr Leydon phoned yesterday and said he would fetch me on Wednesday and drive me to town, and that Mr Arrowsmith would interview me —and hear me—that afternoon. I explained about its being my day for my lesson. But—' she cleared her throat nervously—'it appeared this was Mr Arrowsmith's only time for seeing me.'

'Then you had the perfect get-out if you really wanted to avoid any contact with him, didn't you?' Lewis's tone was quiet but not somehow reassuring.

'If you like to look at it that way,' she agreed. 'On the other hand, he is a very influential man——'

'Not in the world of serious music, which is your aim.'

'Are there two such sharply divided worlds of music?' she asked a little irritably because she was nervous.

'Yes, there are. And if you don't know that by now I've been wasting my time,' was the curt reply.

'I don't want you flirting with the kind of plan Max Arrowsmith would have in mind. The sort of thing he promotes is slick, occasionally brilliant but always rather cheap. It's not for you.'

'Jerome Leydon seems to think very highly of him,' she replied resentfully. 'I think he even has some hand in whatever it is Mr Arrowsmith has in mind.'

'Very possibly. Though he is a highly talented man I imagine he has few artistic principles. Is he an admirer of yours?'

'Musically, do you mean?'

'No. Personally.'

'Of course not! What a ridiculous idea.'

'Not a ridiculous idea at all. He apparently hangs around after you, even comes to church to hear you, and now wants to promote what he regards as your best interests with his tough friend Max Arrowsmith. He also seems perfectly able to whisk you off to London to hear concerts or audition for Arrowsmith or any-anything else without much effort at refusal on your part. You should never have let him talk you into this questionable venture. It would have been much easier to refuse in the first instance. You'll probably find it difficult to do so now.'

'But I don't propose to refuse.' Amanda felt her temper rising.

'If you wish to remain my student you will have to do so,' he replied almost casually; and it was a second before the full implication of that hit her.

'You can't seriously mean that?' she gasped.

'Certainly I mean it. You don't suppose I've been giving you lessons all this time so that Max Arrowsmith, of all people, should reap the rewards by putting you into one of his contemptible shows?'

'Are you throwing it up at me that I had all those lessons free?' she retorted furiously.

'No, my dear, I'm doing nothing of the kind—and well you know it. I'm not putting any financial value on those lessons or their result. If you think that——'

'I don't think it!' she interrupted quickly and remorsefully. 'I had no right to say such a thing. It was just that I was furious you could be so—high-handed.'

'All right, I accept that.' He sounded as though he meant it. 'And I don't want you ever to feel under any obligation to me because I've taught you all this time. I'm looking at the whole thing as a sort of act of creation in which both of us have played a part. Sit down, Mandy——' for she had risen to her feet during the discussion.

She dropped into the nearest chair and he went on quite calmly and reasonably, as though he were explaining to an intelligent but difficult child.

'Have you ever thought just what a voice is, physically speaking? It's simply air passing through vocal chords. The voice will vary of course according to the quality of those chords. But until intelligence and dedication and artistry are brought to bear upon it, it will have little importance or individuality. Someone has to teach the owner of those chords what to do, and an enormous amount of work and dedication will be required from both teacher and pupil. You've played your part admirably, Mandy —I grant you that. I've never had a pupil who worked harder or with more devotion. On my side I've tried to impart to you everything I have and am as a true musician. The result, though not yet quite complete, looks like justifying all we've done together. Do you seriously suppose that I'm going to let Max Arrowsmith mix *his* coarse handiwork with ours? I forbid you to keep that appointment with him.'

'You—forbid me?' she repeated incredulously, and she stared at him as he leaned back almost negligently against the piano and regarded her.

'Yes.'

She wanted to ask by what right he presumed to forbid her. But she knew. He had already explained. If she were ever going to be a singer, she was partly his creation. He was, one might almost say, fighting for his part in her.

'All right,' she heard herself say slowly. 'I won't go to London on Wednesday.'

Only then did she realise, by the way his body relaxed, how tensely he had been holding himself in check while appearing to regard her almost indifferently.

'Good girl,' was all Lewis said. But as he passed her on his way out of the church schoolroom she was stupefied to realise that he bent over her and dropped a seemingly careless kiss on the top of her head.

She sat there motionless for some minutes after he had gone. She would not be seeing him again until he was in the church, playing the organ for Evensong, and she was in her place in the choir. In other words, there was no prospect of any further talk between them on the subject which so profoundly affected her life. She could not take back her promise to cancel the proposed trip to London on Wednesday. The matter was closed so far as he was concerned. Her task now—and a most unwelcome one it seemed to her at that moment—was to explain to Jerome Leydon that she was withdrawing from any involvement with Max Arrowsmith.

To say that her thoughts wandered during the evening service would be largely true. Only the professional and disciplined part of her was fully engaged with the music, her private reflections having little to do with what was happening around her. But from time to time she glanced over at the back of the man sitting at the organ, and she asked herself why she felt so bound to follow any advice, or order, that he cared to give.

As she had expected, he said no more than the general 'goodnight' which he addressed to all his choir at the end of the evening. Then he went off home and Amanda mounted her bicycle and rode slowly back to The Nightingale, reflecting on the disagreeable explanations which lay ahead of her.

It was not just a question of breaking the news to Jerome. There would be Nan—and to a much lesser degree her brother—who would need to be convinced that she was acting wisely. Not that Henry would bring the slightest pressure to bear on her, even verbally. It was Nan who would be difficult. Nan, whose vicarious pride and pleasure in recent developments had been so touchingly unexpected. As though, instead of envying her young sister-in-law her good fortune, she warmed her own frozen ambitions at the glow of Amanda's bright prospects.

'I wish I'd never told her about Jerry's phone call,' Amanda thought discontentedly. 'Then I wouldn't have to explain about my changed decision. Oh, well, I suppose I'd better get the explanations over right away. No point in delaying things. If Henry is there——'

But Henry was not there when she came in. Nan was sitting alone in the family dining room, some

account books before her on the table; although, as
Amanda reflected in passing, those books were
usually Henry's concern.

'Henry gone to bed already?' she enquired.

'Yes. He didn't feel too good.' Nan did not look
up as she replied. She just pushed back her hair
from her forehead with a weary gesture, and it
struck Amanda suddenly that her sister-in-law's
voice was slightly husky.

'Is anything wrong?' she enquired quickly.

'Well—no, not *wrong* exactly.' Nan glanced up
then and Amanda exclaimed incredulously,

'Nan!—you've been crying. What's the matter?
Is Henry ill again?'

'No.' Nan shook her head slowly. 'He's no worse
than he's been during the last year or so. That's to
say, he tires easily, has a good deal of pain—and
never complains. The problem is not that he's worse.
The problem is that he could be very much better—
if only we could afford it.'

'Afford it? But of course we can afford it—*must*
afford it, if he could really be helped and made much
better,' Amanda exclaimed. 'What's the trouble,
Nan?' She sat down opposite her sister-in-law and
put out her hand across the table. 'I thought we were
doing so well.'

'We are doing well, comparatively speaking.'
Oddly enough, Nan ignored the outstretched hand,
almost as though she could not bring herself to
accept Amanda's eager gesture of comfort. 'But
we're not in a position to face really big expense—
or reorganisation.' She hesitated a moment and then,
as though forcing herself, she went on, 'I'd better
explain. You remember that Swiss doctor and his
wife who stayed here some months ago?'

'Yes. Doctor Charole, wasn't it? He got on so well with Henry. They talked a lot together, I remember.'

'He was very much interested in Henry's case. Since then he's kept in touch by letter, and recently —about ten days ago—he wrote with the proposition that Henry should go out to his clinic near Berne. What he suggests is an operation and long post-operative treatment. Four months—perhaps six. Both he and the colleagues he has consulted are ninety per cent certain there could be at best an almost complete cure, at worst a great improvement in Henry's state of health. Without some such treatment there could be serious deterioration in a year or two.'

Amanda passed the tip of her tongue over suddenly dry lips and asked hoarsely, 'Is it madly expensive?—the operation and treatment, I mean.'

'For what's involved, frankly no. Dr Charole has made a very generous offer. But on any terms it would involve more than we could possibly raise. In addition to which, while Henry was away for an indefinite period, we should have to engage a salaried assistant to replace him.'

'Of course, of course,' Amanda murmured, and then fell silent. But presently she glanced at the account books on the table and said slowly, 'You've been trying to find a way of managing? You've been going into everything while Henry is out of the way. Is that it?'

Nan nodded and then, again in that strangely husky voice, she said, 'He won't consider it himself. I was ready even to bring Clive back from boarding school and send him to school locally. But Henry said it would be insane to mess up his education like that, even if the saving of money would be sufficient

—which it wouldn't. And of course he's right.'

'Yes, he's right,' Amanda agreed absently, while thoughts and plans began to revolve in her mind in a confused and somehow frightening way.

'Henry says we must thank Dr Charole for his generous offer but turn it down as totally impossible,' Nan's husky voice went on. 'Unless—' she cleared her throat nervously—'unless some sort of miracle happens in the family finances.'

A slight chill rippled down Amanda's spine. But she said steadily, 'That's why you were so interested in Max Arrowsmith and his plans, isn't it?'

Again Nan nodded. Then she burst out suddenly, 'It's unfair, I know, to involve you and your fortunes so shamelessly in our affairs, but——'

'It's not unfair at all,' interrupted Amanda firmly. 'I'm Henry's sister, just as you're Henry's wife. We both love him and——'

'That's it,' Nan interrupted in her turn, with a sort of heartbreaking simplicity. 'I love him—I *love* Henry. I know I'm sometimes short-tempered and hateful and impatient when things get on top of me. But that's just on the surface, Mandy—truly it is. Underneath all that he's still the man I fell in love with, and I'd do anything—anything for him. I'd commit a crime for him, I think, if it really would help.' She laughed shortly, a laugh which suddenly turned into dreadful little sobs, and she wept and wept uncontrollably, while Amanda stared at her in horrified unbelief before trying, in broken sentences, to offer some form of comfort.

CHAPTER FIVE

For a few panic-stricken moments Amanda stared in wordless dismay at her sister-in-law. Then, as Nan strove to regain her composure, the sobs subsided into small hiccuping sounds, strangely like a child and so totally unlike her usual well-controlled self that Amanda could have wept in her turn.

'I'm sorry. I don't know what's the matter with me,' Nan muttered.

'I do,' said Amanda gently. 'You've been carrying an intolerable burden far too long. And now to have had some real hope dangled before you and then withdrawn is just about all anyone could take.'

'Maybe.' Almost indifferently Nan scrubbed her damp handkerchief across her ravaged face. Well—' she began to pile the account books together—'there's nothing much else to say.'

But Amanda put out a hand to stop her.

'Listen, Nan. There's quite a lot more to say. It would be stupid to build any extravagant hopes on what Max Arrowsmith hinted. But at least he wants to see and hear me, and I'm to be taken there by someone who passionately wants him to engage me. I don't know any more than you do what he may have in mind. But now that I understand the family situation I'm going to strain every nerve to get a good offer out of him. If I do, then no one—' she pushed the thought of Lewis Elsworth from her mind—'and nothing is going to stop me from accepting it.'

'Oh, Mandy! If only——' Nan broke off with a

sigh. Then, as though her thoughts had made a complete switch, she asked suddenly, 'What did Dr Elsworth say when you told him you were going to London to see Max Arrowsmith?'

'He more or less forbade me to go,' replied Amanda with an astonishing assumption of carelessness. 'But I couldn't accept that, of course. I must be free to make my own decisions when it comes to essentials.'

'Of course.' Nan shot a curious glance at her. 'Did he agree to that in the end?'

'No, he didn't.' Amanda made herself smile, as though she recalled the scene with a touch of amusement. 'In fact, he threatened to stop my lessons. But he wouldn't really do that, you know. He was just flexing his muscles a bit and hoping to scare me, I imagine.'

'How horrid of him!' Nan made a slight face. 'Anyway,' she added reflectively, 'if Mr Arrowsmith did offer you something worthwhile you probably wouldn't need any more lessons from Dr Elsworth, would you?'

'Possibly not,' agreed Amanda, feeling as though someone had stabbed her.—Or was it she who had done the stabbing? It would be difficult to say which, she thought, as she bade Nan goodnight and turned away.

'Don't you want some supper?' her sister-in-law asked in surprise. 'It's early yet.'

'I know.' Amanda stifled an impulse to say the very thought of food made her feel sick. Then, as Nan continued to look questioningly at her, she said, 'Maybe I'll have some milk.' And, going into the kitchen, she helped herself to a glass of milk and stood by the window, looking out into the gathering dusk, as she slowly drank it.

Suddenly, with great clarity, she recalled that day when Oscar Warrender and his wife had driven up to the little hotel and she had heard Anthea say. 'It's called The Nightingale. Isn't that charmingly appropriate?' and how later he had explained that it was appropriate because they were looking for a young singer who lived in the district. Herself.

'Another world,' Amanda thought with a sigh. 'Or it will be if Max Arrowsmith decides that he wants to engage me. But I have no choice. Not now I know about Henry. Lewis won't understand, of course. Nothing would make him understand. He's rooted in his own prejudices—principles—whatever one likes to call them. And how on earth do I tell him that, after all, I *am* going to audition for Arrowsmith?'

That was the overruling question now in her mind. And then she realised that 'tell' was not the right word. She simply could not face further argument with him, whether in person or by telephone.

'I'll write instead,' she decided with a sort of cowardly sense of relief. 'I'll write and say——' She continued to stand there in the darkening kitchen and began to compose her letter in her mind. It was not easy. The more she thought of explanations the feebler they became. In the end she went up to her bedroom, took out paper and pen and simply wrote:

'Dear Lewis, I am very sorry but circumstances beyond my control have forced me to change my decision. I *am* going to London after all to see Max Arrowsmith. Please believe me when I say that I hate to oppose your wishes. I shall not be coming to my Wednesday lesson nor to choir practice, but I hope to give you some sort of explanation on Sunday. Sincerely and gratefully, Amanda.'

It seemed pretty thin and foolish when she read it

over, and it seemed little better when she re-read it in the morning. But nothing more brilliant came to her mind and so she posted the letter on Tuesday, determined that he should receive it in time to realise she was not coming, though not in sufficient time to interfere in any way with her change of plans.

To her brother she said nothing of what she now knew and Nan, as though sensing that even one word out of place might alter the delicate balance of the situation, also made no further reference to the subject. Indeed, she was so much her usual self that Amanda wondered uneasily how often in the past she had hidden anguish and anxiety behind a cool exterior.

Only on the Wednesday morning did Nan ask briefly, 'What time is Jerome coming to fetch you?' And she drew a slight but audible sigh of relief when Amanda replied equally briefly, 'About two-thirty.'

She was ready and waiting when he arrived and knew immediately from his quick, comprehensive glance of approval that he was more than satisfied with her appearance.

'You look enchanting,' he told her as she took her seat beside him in the car. 'Just the right note. They can't fail to be impressed.'

'They?' She glanced at him questioningly. 'I thought it was just you and Mr Arrowsmith.'

'No, no——' he laughed that off quite casually. 'There are two or three people involved in this enterprise. Including me, as I told you on the phone.'

'Would you like to tell me a little more about what you call this enterprise?' She tried to keep the dry note out of her voice but was aware, from his quick glance, that she had not succeeded in doing so.

'I'm sorry if I've seemed a bit secretive.' He was

his usual warm, expansive self now. 'But in show business one remains a little cagey until everything is signed and sealed. There's always the risk that one's most deadly rival will beat you to the post otherwise. But I can tell you that what we are considering is something between a sophisticated musical—sharp, witty and provocative—and what might be described as a music drama. It's stronger—more frank and earthy—than the usual musical frolic and requires a very definite type of heroine. You, in fact, if I have my way and if you please Max and his associates.'

Amanda considered the term 'frank and earthy', found it singularly unattractive, but resisted the desire to question it at this point. Instead she asked, 'Have you written all the music for this work?'

'I have.'

'But it's not exactly an opera?'

'Oh, no!' He laughed at the idea. 'It's directed at quite a different type of audience. More sophisticated, more lively, I suppose one might say.'

Reluctantly she recalled Lewis's dictum on Jerome Leydon—'Though a highly talented man he has few artistic principles.' And after a short silence she asked, 'Do I—I mean does the heroine—come out as what you call a sophisticated type?'

'No, no.' He laughed again at that. 'She is the innocent—charming innocent, of course—to whom everything happens. I can just see and hear you in the part. That lovely fresh—yes, innocent—sound in your voice is ideal for it.'

'Meaning that I shall be called on to look and sound a fool?' she suggested, setting her teeth.

'No, dear, no.' He took a hand from the wheel and patted hers reassuringly. 'There's a sort of amusing purity about the character. It's difficult to describe. You have to *hear* it for yourself. You'll love the music. It's eminently singable—about the best thing I've ever done, and I can't wait to hear you try out some of it. Don't look so solemn, love. If you get the part—and I'm determined that you shall—you'll be a riot on the first night. Now smile for me. It's a chance most girls would give a lot to have.'

She smiled then. What else could she do? If Lewis had not spoken so forcefully against *any* Max Arrowsmith proposal she would not now be entertaining these nagging doubts. She would be feeling happy and elated. She was not forced to accept—and certainly not to adopt—all Lewis's prejudices. Jerome was right: most girls would jump at such a chance. She too must be ready to jump, if indeed the chance were offered to her.

After that the subject was firmly changed by her companion and not referred to again during the rest of the drive. Even when they arrived at the magnificent block from which Max Arrowsmith apparently directed his personal empire Jerome gave her little chance to question or comment. On the contrary, glancing at his watch and muttering something about being only just on time, he hurried her into an ornate lift which silently whisked them up to what appeared to be the top floor of the building. As she stepped out into a thickly carpeted corridor Amanda saw that the door of the room at the end was open and from the room came the sound of several voices.

Without explanation or preamble Jerome conducted her into the room where half a dozen men and one woman were grouped round a table talking. They all stopped as Amanda and her companion entered and Jerome simply said, 'Here she is,' and gave her the slightest push to indicate that she was to go forward.

She knew instinctively that even this first approach was curiously important and suddenly she found herself thinking of Henry and not at all of Lewis. She went towards the table with an air of slightly timid purpose, smiled a little tentatively at the ring of faces, then looked full at Max Arrowsmith who was watching her from the head of the table and said with a quiet air of composure which surprised herself, 'Good afternoon, Mr Arrowsmith. Thank you for arranging to see me.'

'Thank *you*, my dear,' was the reply as Arrowsmith got to his feet, and she knew, though she could not have said why, that he was pleased with her. 'I'm not going to make any introductions at this point. Just think of us as interested members of your audience. We would like to hear you sing before we discuss anything else. Miss Mead—' he indicated the one woman present—'will take you to the audition room. There's no hurry. Take your time and relax. If you're tired after your journey—'

'Oh, but I couldn't be, you know,' said Amanda. 'I was brought here by car. I'm used to cycling most places.'

One or two of the men laughed at that and Miss Mead rose from the table and said, 'Come with me.' Then she led Amanda from the room and along the corridor to a small hall with a platform at one end.

'Let them wait ten minutes,' she said in an unexpectedly deep and husky voice. 'It does them good and whets their appetite. I'm playing for you. My name's Josephine, by the way. Are you a good sight-reader?'

'Pretty good.' Amanda felt curiously unafraid, as though she had plunged into an unknown stream from which there was now no turning back. She must do her best to swim, but if she sank—she sank. 'Do I have to start right off by sight-reading?' she enquired.

'No. I suggest you begin with something in which you're totally at home and which you know you sing well. Let them have the full impact of any vocal attainments you may have. What are you used to singing?'

'Oratorio mostly,' Amanda admitted. At which Josephine Mead laughed, not unkindly, and said,

'Well, that's a novelty in this place anyway. I doubt if any of them have even heard the Hallelujah Chorus. Except Arrowsmith, of course. He knows more than he lets on. Did you bring any music?'

Amanda proffered the small assortment she had brought and Miss Mead unhesitatingly picked out 'Hear ye, Israel' and asked, 'Can you really sing this? —well, I mean.'

'Sir Oscar Warrender seemed to think so,' replied Amanda coolly, and the other woman gave her a speculative glance and remarked,

'Well, either this audition is going to be a sensation or you're going to fall flat on your face. Shall I call them in to hear you now?'

'Yes.' Amanda slipped off her coat, piled her things almost carelessly on a vacant chair and went to stand in the curve of the grand piano.

Presently the others came sauntering in, still talking, and she noticed that Jerome looked distinctly nervous. Then when they were seated she said with astonishing composure, 'I don't know quite what you wanted me to sing, gentlemen, but I'm going to sing

"Hear ye, Israel" from Mendelssohn's *Elijah* because I know it well and it shows off any voice I have.'

'Never heard of it,' observed the man sitting next to Arrowsmith in a disparaging tone.

'No, you wouldn't have,' replied Arrowsmith coolly. 'It's not your line of country. Go ahead, Amanda.'

So Josephine Mead played the introductory bars and even as Amanda began to sing she found her thoughts switch abruptly from her brother and his desperate need to Lewis Elsworth and the long, patient, inspired work he had lavished on her training. It was inevitable, really. Everything about this particular air was associated with him. The almost faultless technique upon which she was even now relying was of his making. She was partly his creation —and she knew that in some obscure way she was betraying him.

Nothing in her voice showed what was in her mind and heart: her musical discipline was too good for that. But even while her voice almost caressed the rising phrases of hope and confidence a fearful sense of self-disgust crept over her. At the end she just stood there, leaning now against the piano, and stared unhappily at the ground until she heard someone say,

'It's a fine tune, but too much repetition. We couldn't use that.'

'We were not thinking of using it,' Jerome cut in contemptuously. 'We're just assessing Amanda's voice.'

'Which is extraordinarily good,' put in the man beside Max Arrowsmith. 'But not sexy, of course. Pity. It's not a bit sexy. Otherwise it's real pretty.'

'She doesn't have to be sexy, if you remember,' Arrowsmith said smoothly. 'She's the one person in the piece who has to be essentially something else.'

A certain amount of discussion broke out at that, and then Jerome interrupted impatiently, 'Let's hear her do some of the first act music.' He came up to the platform and whispered to her, 'Don't look so down-hearted, darling. They're impressed, I can see that. It's just they're a bit bewildered by your choice. But Arrowsmith thinks you're a knock-out. I know the signs when he's really excited—which is almost never. Come and try some of this. You sight-read quite well, don't you?'

She nodded wordlessly and came to stand beside him at the piano, where he took the seat which Josephine Mead had now vacated. As Jerome handed her some sheets of manuscript music Amanda saw that his hand was trembling slightly and she found it in her heart to be sorry for him. After all, this was terribly important to him too, she supposed. And to Henry. She must not forget Henry—or Nan, who had cried so bitterly as she abandoned any hope of helping her husband.

'Glance through it. Take your time.' Jerome's voice was slightly hoarse. 'No, you can keep those sheets with you——' as she went to hand them back. 'I don't need the music. I know it. After all, I wrote it.' He laughed slightly and again she knew that he was nervous.

As she studied the sheets of music Amanda thought she detected some considerable charm and real melody in the phrases. The words were not particularly engaging, but she had little time to take in their exact meaning. Then after a few minutes she said, 'I can manage, I think. Does she really mean what she's singing, Jerry? Is it gay and positive—or is she wistful and uncertain?'

'A little of both. Clever of you to realise the double meaning.' He smiled brilliantly at her. 'Now try it out.'

So she straightened up, faced her hard-boiled audience and braced herself to do full justice to Jerome's composition. She owed him that at least.

There was, as she had thought, considerable melodic charm to the music and, indeed, as she sang it she was reminded irresistibly of the delightful air she had sung that time at school when she had first met him. There was no question of his outstanding talent for inventing tunes which people would delight to sing, nor of his unusual capacity for investing them with a special elegance which was all their own. She realised that some of the words and phrases she was singing had an odd double meaning. They were—she supposed questionable was the word. But with her mind concentrated on her singing she had no time for close analysis.

At the end there was a good deal of comment— most of it complimentary—and then Jerome launched into a duet in which he himself sang with her in a light, undistinguished but pleasing baritone. After which Max Arrowsmith broke up proceedings, gave Amanda an approving nod and said to Miss Mead,

'See that Miss Lovett has whatever she likes in the way of refreshment.' And the men went back to their conference room and Amanda was conducted to yet another room—a small and pleasant place, something between an office and a sitting room, where tea and sandwiches and attractive little cakes were brought in on a tray.

'You did well,' Josephine Mead informed her as

she poured out the tea. 'You realised that, didn't you?'

'I don't know. Not very much was said.'

'Very little *is* said on these occasions in front of the person most concerned,' was the knowledgeable reply. 'But I've been present at so many of them that I can assess the reaction pretty accurately. You walked well, stood well, sang well and gave a very engaging impression. My guess is that all of that adds up to what they're looking for. Does the thought excite you?'

'No,' said Amanda. 'I need the job, but I don't want it. I suppose that sounds rather ridiculous to you?'

'Not specially.—Have a sandwich. They're good. Everything in this place is good—materially speaking.'

Amanda glanced up quickly and asked with sudden candour, 'Why do you work here?'

'For the same reason that you will accept what they offer. I need the job, but I don't want it. What I wanted was to be a concert pianist——'

'You play awfully well,' Amanda interrupted sincerely.

'But not well enough. I'm good, like hundreds of others, but not good enough. I make an excellent living here, doing things I rather despise.' She yawned slightly. 'None of it has anything to do with real music. But in the end you have to come to terms with things as they are and not as you would wish them to be, don't you?'

Amanda looked at her more closely, passed the tip of her tongue over dry lips and asked, 'Why are you telling me all this?'

'I don't know—except that you asked me. But if you repeat any of it to that lot in there I'll deny it and say you're a liar. I need my good job.'

'I shouldn't dream of repeating a word,' Amanda replied. 'But, Josephine—you said I could call you Josephine, didn't you?—do you know much about this work they're all discussing? Have you seen the whole score? And if so, what's it *really* like?'

'I know it quite well. I've had to accompany quite a number of applicants for the various roles. None of them could sing half as well as you. But none of them showed your reluctance to snatch at any chance that offered. The music is very good on its own terms. Not the best that Jerome can do. But then that's Jerome, isn't it, when the rewards are high?'

'I don't know.' Amanda's attention was riveted, for she detected a note of personal bitterness in that last remark which interested her. 'I'm not worried about the music. That has a standard of its own, even if Jerome could really do better things. But I've a feeling of uneasiness about other aspects. Some of the words seemed——' she broke off and the other woman said drily,

'Oh, they are! The situations are amusing if you like that sort of thing, but questionable to the point of making half the audience gasp and the other half roar with laughter. You might persuade them to alter the wording of your own part a little. After all, you're playing the innocent among the rest; the dove among the jays, if you like. But I can't see them listening very sympathetically to the kind of protest you would make. One thing, however—' she narrowed her eyes suddenly—'don't let them jazz up the air you sang—"Hear ye, Israel". I could see the idea in Terence Edgar's eye while you were singing it, and he's devilishly clever at that sort of thing.'

'Over my dead body!' exclaimed Amanda furiously.

'Well, you'll need to be tough. You aren't going to like this, Amanda. Do you need the job *very* badly?'

'Desperately.'

'I see. Play your cards close to your chest, as the saying is. They'll be calling you in soon to make an offer—at least, that's my guess. It will be a good offer, but hedge if you can. Say you must think it over, consult your grandmother, or whatever you like, and don't be stampeded into any kind of commitment. Not even a general one without signatures attached. They'd all back each other up later, even Jerome. It's some time since they started looking for someone like you, and a good deal of money depends on their making an early beginning, with the right person.'

Sudden panic gripped Amanda at that point and, rising to her feet, she exclaimed, 'I don't even want to discuss it, after all. I'm going to slip off *now*, before they can come badgering me.'

'No, you can't do that.' The other woman moved her chair carelessly so that she more or less blocked the way to the door. 'Arrowsmith at least would guess I'd been talking out of turn, and I can't afford that. Don't panic. Just be slow in answering and dither a little. They expect you to be a bit of a goop anyway. I think one of them is coming to call you now. Remember no one can actually force you—not even here. Just say as little as you possibly can. Remember that.'

Amanda remembered it. She remembered it all through the lengthy discussion which followed, during which she was made an offer so handsome that she gasped, even though Josephine had told her it would be good. With an immense effort she wrenched her mind away from the thought of what all that money could do for Henry, for Nan, for the hotel—even for herself. It occurred to her for a confusing moment that perhaps she was being a perfect fool even to consider rejecting what might well be the greatest chance of her life. Was it not possible that Josephine—unknown to her an hour ago—was just an ill-wishing, jealous woman who wanted to spoil her chances? Such people did exist. And there had been peculiar bitterness in the way she spoke of Jerome.

Jerome who said more than once, 'But, darling, why do you have to go home and think it over? It's the sort of offer most girls would give——'

'I'm not most girls,' she replied obstinately. 'I'm myself. And I'm confused and stunned by all that's happening. I have to think it over.'

'You wouldn't be silly enough to chew it over with Lewis Elsworth, would you?' he asked suspiciously.

'No.' She shook her head. 'I just refuse to make up my mind here and now. Mr Arrowsmith—' with sudden inspiration she turned to him—'will you please stop them all badgering me? I thought I came here to sing to *you*.'

'No one wants to badger you, my dear.' He smiled almost reassuringly. 'We're thinking of your own good—and ours too, I admit. How long do you want to think it over?'

'Twenty-four hours,' she said flatly. 'And I want to go now, please.' She stood up. 'No, Jerry—' as he made a move to accompany her—'I don't want you or anyone else with me. I'm going home by train—and alone. Good afternoon, everyone. And thank you for hearing me and making this offer.'

She turned on her heel then and walked out of the room. As she went she heard one of the men say, 'She's a natural for the part. We just have to have her.'

'And who is she going to consult now, for God's sake?' exclaimed another voice which she thought was Jerry's.

Presumably the others only shrugged, for it was Josephine who answered, with a touch of amused malice, 'Oscar Warrender, perhaps.'

The last thing she heard was a burst of laughter as she stepped into the lift and pressed the button for it to descend.

Oscar Warrender. The name fell on her ear with a peculiar sort of significance and, as the lift deposited her silently and discreetly at the ground floor and she went into the busy sunlit street, she asked herself if Josephine had been jeering—or hinting something when she uttered that name so clearly.

'If I knew where he lived,' Amanda muttered, 'I almost think——'

And there, straight before her—almost as though something other than her own will were directing her —there loomed a red telephone booth. It was unoccupied and, dangling by a chain from the shelf, was a shabby directory.

Her hands were not quite steady as she riffled through the pages devoted to the W's, and she felt both scared and triumphant as the name 'Warrender, Sir Oscar' started out at her. Killigrew Mansions, St James's. She stared through the windows of the telephone booth, trying to reorientate herself, and presently it dawned on her that she was scarcely more than ten minutes' walk away. If she went now——

She stepped out into the street again, her breath

coming in short, uneasy little gasps, and though she tried to tell herself that she might do no more than go and look at the place, a sort of desperate resolution was growing within her. It did not occur to her that other anxious singers must have approached that same address with beating hearts at various times. She was only aware of the beating of her own heart and the strange numbness in her brain, which made it impossible for her to think of a plausible sentence with which to account for her presence to whatever servant should open the door.

No such sentence was required, however, when it came to the point. The person who opened the door was Warrender himself and he said. 'Oh——?' as though he had been expecting someone else. And then, not specially welcomingly, 'Elsworth's protégée, isn't it? Did you want to see me or my wife?'

'You,' replied Amanda so huskily that she felt he must be mentally according her poor marks for her diction.

'Well, come in.' He held the door open for her and added, 'The studio is straight ahead. I have only ten or fifteen minutes, I'm afraid.'

'Thank you.' She managed to make that a little clearer. 'It's good of you to allow me even a short time without an appointment.'

She had the impression that he thought so too, though he did not put it into words. He indicated a chair, sat down opposite her and asked with disconcerting abruptness, 'Well, what is it?'

That was the moment when she knew she should never have come. How *did* one explain the terrible complications of her dilemma in ten or fifteen minutes? She had not even arranged her thoughts, let alone the words in which to clothe them.

There was a frightful pause. Then she blurted out, 'I want—I need—your advice.'

He looked bored and enquired not very kindly, 'Artistically, morally or financially?'

'I suppose—all three,' she said, astonished to realise that this was more or less the case; and she felt she could hardly blame him when he replied irritably, 'But why come to me, for heaven's sake?'

'Because you probably know the answer better than anyone else.' And suddenly her mind cleared miraculously. 'I've been made an offer—an extremely good offer—to play the lead in one of Max Arrowsmith's shows. I need the money desperately because my brother is ill and requires expensive medical help which might cure him.'

'And you're asking me what you should do?'

Amanda nodded.

'You reject Arrowsmith's offer out of hand. God gave you a beautiful and unusual voice—I will tell you that much. Your teacher has put his heart and soul into seeing that it is properly developed, refined and cared for. It is now your responsibility. If you go selling it to anyone like Arrowsmith, you will be untrue to your art, your teacher and your Maker.'

'But what about Henry?—what about my brother?'

'Will he die if he doesn't have this treatment?'

'No, not that. But he could be made so much better if——'

'He'll find the money somehow. There are always ways,' replied Warrender with the careless certainty of someone who has never experienced acute money difficulties. 'A mortgage on that charming hotel or——'

'No, no, it's not as simple as that,' cried Amanda

distractedly, with a sudden recollection of Nan and the account books. 'You see——'

'No, my dear, I don't see.' And at that he stood up with the obvious indication that the interview was at an end. 'You've asked my advice and I've given it to you. That's all I can do.'

She also got to her feet then, but a little unsteadily. She knew she had failed. What had seemed a wonderful idea at first was nothing more than the feeble grasping at a straw as one went down for the third time.

'I'm sorry—to have troubled you,' she said mechanically, and made for the door which suddenly seemed a long way off.

But before she could reach it someone else opened it from the outside: an elderly maid who stood in the doorway and addressed Sir Oscar respectfully.

'Dr Elsworth is here, sir,' she said. 'Shall I show him in or ask him to wait in the music-room?'

CHAPTER SIX

OSCAR WARRENDER was not a man to hesitate about his decisions. He said to the maid, 'Show in Dr Elsworth,' at precisely the same moment as Amanda breathed a protesting, 'Oh, no!'

The maid very properly took this to be an independent exclamation on the visitor's part and nothing so presumptuous as a countermanding of her employer's order. She withdrew and Warrender said to Amanda, 'You'd better sit down again.'

'But I'd rather not see Dr Elsworth. At least— not now.'

'You haven't much choice,' was the reply as the door opened once more and Lewis Elsworth was ushered in. He came towards Warrender with a smile and an outstretched hand. But the smile faded and the hand dropped to his side as he took in the other occupant of the room and, instead of addressing the conductor, he said sharply, 'Amanda! What are you doing here?'

'She came to consult me about something,' explained Sir Oscar in an unusually mild tone of voice. 'It was purely coincidental that she and you chose the same afternoon. Do you mind if Anthea joins the discussion? I think she would be interested.' And without waiting for any comment from either Lewis or Amanda—should they have had any to make which seemed doubtful—he went to the door and called, 'Darling!'

Even then it vaguely surprised Amanda that he

should use such a term to anyone. But Anthea Warrender came immediately at his summons, greeted
Lewis with a friendly air and then, suddenly noticing
Amanda's presence, said, 'Hello! What a good idea
for you to come too.'

'We didn't come together,' stated Lewis stiffly.

'No?' Anthea looked questioning and slightly
amused. It was her husband who explained with
characteristic brevity, 'Miss Amanda came to consult me on a professional problem, and Lewis happened to arrive ten minutes early for our appointment.'

'May I ask what the professional problem was?'
enquired Lewis, still in that stiff way which Amanda
found both infuriating and intimidating. But when
Warrender glanced enquiringly at her she made a
helpless little gesture of assent.

'Amanda—' he left out the 'Miss' this time—'has
been made a very tempting offer by Max Arrowsmith——'

'I told her she was to have nothing to do with the
man,' interrupted Lewis furiously. 'His enterprises
are totally outside anything I have—I had—in mind
for her.'

Amanda noted the significant change of tense with
a sort of chilled dismay, for it implied so clearly that
his plans for her no longer existed.

'Could we know what the tempting offer was?'
Anthea asked with genuine curiosity, and as she
addressed Amanda directly, it was Amanda who was
forced to reply.

'He's promoting some sort of musical drama,' she
said huskily. 'Jerome Leydon has composed the
music—which is good of its kind. They and their—
their professional associates want me to sing the lead-

ing role. I suppose you might say that I auditioned
for them this afternoon.'

'And what,' enquired Warrender with interest, 'did
you sing for them at your audition?'

'I first sang "Hear ye, Israel" and then——'

Until that moment it had never occurred to
Amanda that the famous conductor could laugh so
heartily. Nor that he could look so extraordinarily
attractive as he did so. The clear-cut, austere features
relaxed unexpectedly and the uncomfortably pene-
trating eyes sparkled with delighted amusement.
Anthea also laughed after a moment. But Lewis,
Amanda noticed, remained completely serious. Even
when Warrender said,

'Good lord, Elsworth, don't you find it *funny* that
she sang "Hear ye, Israel" to that bunch?'

'No,' replied Lewis shortly, 'I don't find it funny at
all. It's like someone showing herself off in a slave
market in the hope of interesting the highest bidder.'

'How dare you!' Amanda sprang to her feet. 'You
don't understand in the slightest degree. You don't
even want to understand. All you want to do is sit in
judgment on people and despise them if they don't
conform to your own little set of rules. I didn't go to
Arrowsmith because I wanted to. I hated every
minute I spent there, if you'd like to know. I felt sick,
but——'

'But you accepted his offer?' said Lewis softly.

'No, I did not. I said—I *had* to say—that I would
think it over. Then, when I came out into the street,
I had a sort of inspiration. I decided to go to Sir
Oscar and ask his advice.'

'You didn't think my advice—which I'd already
given you—was sufficient?'

'No, I didn't. Because you were not in a position

to judge. You knew only half the story. The other half is that my brother, who is ill and getting progressively worse, has a chance of being made better, but it involves a lot of money and *someone* in the family has got to find it. My sister-in-law has done everything she can. She—she cried when she told me, and you can't imagine what that means. She's so tough—so brave usually: she's had to be. But she loves him—and so do I. You don't understand one bit. Neither of you!' The glance she shot at Warrender included him in her reproach and contempt. 'You just blather about artistic integrity!'

There was an odd little silence. Then Anthea said, 'Well, since neither of you seems to know what to say I'll ask the sixty-four-thousand-dollar question. How much money is involved, Amanda?'

'I don't quite know.' Amanda passed her hands wearily over her face. 'A lot. He—Henry—has been offered a long course of treatment in Switzerland under a famous specialist who's greatly interested in his case. But that isn't the major expense. The real problem is that Henry would have to be replaced at the hotel by a paid employee, and we simply can't afford it. We've only just begun to break even in the last six months. It's been a tremendous struggle— mostly Nan's struggle. Now there's no one to help but me, and how can I refuse to play my part? He's her husband, it's true. But he's my brother, and *I* love him, just as she does.'

There was a brief silence once more, then, turning to her husband, Anthea asked, 'What advice did you give her, Oscar?'

'To refuse Arrowsmith's offer at all costs,' he replied shortly.

'Knowing the bit about her brother?' Then, as he

merely shrugged, 'You really are an unsympathetic so-and-so, aren't you? And a bit of humbug too. What would *your* artistic integrity rate, I wonder, if you had to balance it against my health and happiness?'

'Virtually nothing,' replied Warrender with unexpected candour. And the anger went from her eyes and she lightly touched his arm as though in apology.

'All right,' said Anthea. 'If it isn't a terrific sum, Amanda, I'll pay it.'

'And suppose it is a terrific sum?' enquired her husband disagreeably, but he put his hand over hers as it rested on his arm.

'Well then, darling, I'm afraid you'll have to pay it,' Anthea informed him with a smile. 'You can always do a few extra concerts if necessary, can't you?'

'But that,' said Lewis Elsworth unexpectedly, 'leaves me out.' And as they all turned to look at him he cleared his throat and went on, 'Amanda is in some sense my concern. I should naturally—' he began to look uncomfortable and slightly cross—'I should naturally wish to take part in any rescue operation, if one might term it that.'

'I couldn't possibly take your money!' exclaimed Amanda, swallowing a great lump in her throat and resisting a desire to throw her arms round his neck.

'Which of us do you suppose she's addressing?' asked Warrender of no one in particular.

'All of us to a certain degree,' said Anthea. 'But Lewis in particular. Like all nice independent people Amanda naturally winces at the thought of accepting help from anyone. But with Lewis she feels a special obligation because she owes her splendid training to him. However, he really wants to do it, Amanda, anyone can see he does. So don't cry about it, though it's very sweet and moving of him.'

'I'm not *going* to cry,' Amanda insisted with a great effort. 'For one thing—' she laughed shakily —'he says it makes him nervous if I do.'

'Has he made you cry before, then?' enquired Sir Oscar with interest. 'How horrid of him.'

'Listen who's talking!' exclaimed Anthea. 'You made me cry quarts when you were supervising my training. Remember?'

'That's different,' asserted Warrender. 'Let us keep to the main point. Which is, Amanda, that neither I nor Dr Elsworth will hear of your accepting Arrowsmith's proposal, either in your own interests or, possibly, ours. Shall I go on, Elsworth?' He glanced at Lewis, who after a moment said reluctantly, 'Very well.'

'Then why don't we discuss it over tea?' suggested Anthea. 'It would be pleasanter.'

'I—I've already had tea. At Max Arrowsmith's office,' Amanda said apologetically.

'You should never break bread—or drink tea— with the enemy,' Lewis told her perfectly seriously. Then he held out his hand and smiled, and when she put her hand into his he gripped it so hard that he almost hurt her. But she thought no touch of the hand had ever conveyed more comfort to her.

Over tea Sir Oscar reduced the whole situation to startlingly simple terms. 'The practical financial details can be dealt with almost immediately. 'I'll send my accountant to see your brother and sister-in-law, Amanda. They can work out what will be necessary, arrange a substitute for your brother while he's away, see that he goes as soon as possible to—where is it? —Switzerland for his treatment, and Anthea and Lewis and I will decide what we are each contributing. It shouldn't be difficult.'

'Not difficult?' Again Amanda passed her hand over her face in a gesture of bewilderment. 'But only half an hour ago it seemed utterly insoluble. Surely the problem can't be disposed of just like that? It can't be so *simple*?'

'Much simpler than arranging an opera season or tour, I assure you,' replied Warrender with his rare and charming smile. 'Possibly,' he added with a touch of malice, 'simpler than any project Max Arrowsmith had in mind.'

'Particularly now we've removed his trump card,' added Lewis with an air of frank satisfaction. 'What was his rotten show about, Amanda, anyway?'

'I don't think it would be ethical to discuss a proposition I've turned down,' Amanda told him demurely. 'Certainly not with someone who has a rival suggestion to make. For Sir Oscar did say something about its being in your interests as well as mine that I should reject Mr Arrowsmith's offer. Could I hear about that now, please?'

'She wants to decide whether she should turn *us* down,' commented Warrender drily.

'Oh, no!' Amanda exclaimed quickly. 'I couldn't possibly turn down anything you all suggested. Not after what you've offered to do—with such incredible generosity. I want you to understand that. I could never, never repay you all, and I'll do anything you want—any*thing*.'

'That's a bit too rash and expansive of you,' Sir Oscar warned her, but not unkindly, and Anthea gave her a very brilliant smile. Only Lewis looked at the ground and said nothing. Until Amanda, arrested by his silence and his attitude, stared at him and simply *willed* him to look her way. He raised his eyes then and met hers. But in his there was something inscrutable which puzzled and slightly disturbed her, though she did not know why.

'Perhaps you would do the explaining, Sir Oscar,' he said at that point, and then leaned back in his chair as though the conversation no longer concerned him vitally. Amanda was therefore all the more startled when Warrender began, without preamble.

'Our project centres round the fact that I find Lewis has, over the last year or two, composed a considerable amount of very attractive operatic music —but without ever coming to grips with what might be called a basic central theme. There is a lot of beautiful, singable stuff, but not related to anything one could call a strong libretto. In fact, a very odd case of putting the operatic cart before the horse.'

He paused and Amanda said doubtfully, 'But surely one could find a good librettist who would be interested in fashioning a story of some kind? Isn't that sort of thing done sometimes?'

'Without a basic theme? and with a composer unknown to the theatre world?' Warrender shook his head. 'Not an impossibility, I suppose, but too tenuous to interest many people.'

Amanda was silent for several moments, then she said wonderingly, 'Are you asking for my advice?'

'Not really.' The conductor laughed slightly. 'Elsworth says that in some way you have a special understanding of his music and what he calls his artistic philosophy——'

'*I* have?'

Warrender nodded coolly and went on, 'He was coming to discuss the whole position with me this afternoon and I believe intended to bring you into it later. Then he telephoned this morning and said there was no question of involving you. I'm not sure why, but——'

'I know,' Amanda interrupted quickly. 'He knew by then that I was going to consider Arrowsmith's offer. That in fact I'd opted for the——the——' she hesitated for the word and Lewis suddenly supplied it.

'For the dark instead of the light,' he said sombrely and, oddly enough, the curious statement did not sound in the least priggish.

'Exactly,' agreed Amanda without offence. 'That's really the essence of you and the way you regard your music, isn't it? And that's why you couldn't have had anything more to do with my development if I'd accepted Max Arrowsmith's offer. In a strange way perhaps that's the answer—to your present problem.'

She stopped speaking, as though struck by some idea which was still just a little bit beyond her grasp, and no one said a word as she sat there in silence for a whole minute. Then she began to speak slowly again.

'It's only the germ of an idea, but—what they offered me this afternoon was a smart, rather unpleasantly amusing affair in which the one decent character was presented as an attractive naïve sort of dimwit; the innocent to whom everything happened, in fact. I'm pretty sure that by the end she'd learned all their unpleasant ways for herself and proved far more adept at them than anyone else on the stage. It could be very funny to some people, I suppose, but was basically a story of degeneration.'

'Sounds like an Arrowsmith hit,' agreed Warrender drily. 'But what has that to do with our problem?'

'Just that—couldn't one play the process in reverse?' said Amanda diffidently. 'If a witty study in degeneration can be very effective, couldn't a moving study in regeneration be effective too in a different way?'

'Difficult not to make it smug and priggish.' Warrender pulled a slight face. 'And really not in tune with the times, I'm afraid. A high moral tone on the stage was once much admired, but I can't see it making much headway with the so-called intelligentsia today.'

'I didn't mean it like that. I've put it badly.' Amanda gripped her hands together in an effort to make herself clear. 'There's nothing goody-goody about the character I have in mind. She's more someone who starts with few redeeming qualities and by experience and—suffering, I suppose, becomes a fully developed soul.'

'It sounds dangerously evangelistic,' objected Warrender. 'What do you think, Elsworth?'

'Come here to the piano,' Lewis said to Amanda. 'You can read my manuscript and words, can't you? You did so once before.'

'Yes, I think so.' She took the sheets of paper from him, nervously but with a rising sense of excitement. And after a minute or two she asked curiously, 'What *are* these words?'

'They're an ancient prayer for warding off the Evil One,' replied Lewis calmly. 'Sing it.'

So for the second time that day she stood beside a composer, sight-reading what he had written. But the two experiences were awesomely different. Leydon's effort had been charming, scintillating, clever. This was something almost uncanny, deeply moving and expressive of fear and appeal.

At the end Amanda said slowly, 'That's what she sings when she's learned enough of what is right to fear what is wrong.'

'That,' replied Lewis softly, 'is what *you* will sing, my dear. It's your music. I present it to you.'

'Which does not give us a practical libretto,' put in Warrender, but there was an oddly indulgent note in his voice.

'I think,' said Anthea, 'the man we want is Patrick Rogerson. He has a feeling for this sort of thing, but at the same time a real grip of incident and action and the creation of characters with whom one can weep and laugh and agonise.'

'He has no real vein of poetry.' Lewis spoke doubtfully, already prepared, Amanda saw, to do battle for his cherished work.

'The music itself supplies that,' Warrender said. 'I think perhaps Anthea is right. If we don't have someone with a thoroughly practical knowledge of what is theatrically gripping the work could degenerate into one of those high-thinking, theoretical studies invariably described as "interesting". The kiss of death,' he added contemptuously, 'to any enterprise and guaranteed to empty any theatre.'

The others all laughed at that, and the extraordinary degree of tension which had built up in the room relaxed. So much so that Amanda found she could not ask Lewis quite what he had meant when he said it was her music and that she would sing it. He could not possibly, she assured herself, have meant the remark in anything but the most general sense. He was surely not thinking of *casting* her for—well, anything?

At that point Lewis glanced at his watch and exclaimed that he would have to leave in order to catch his train.

'How about you, Amanda? I suppose you were driven to town. Are you driving back?'

'No.' She flushed slightly. 'If I may I'll come with you and catch the same train.'

'You may,' he said, effortlessly restoring the teacher–pupil relationship in a matter of seconds. 'Sir Oscar, I can't thank you enough for your help and support. May I leave it to you and your wife to contact Rogerson and find out if he's interested?'

'Of course.' The Warrenders both came to the door to bid goodbye to Amanda and Lewis. And with the air of a man who was used to pulling all the strings, Sir Oscar said to Lewis, 'If Rogerson is interested I'll arrange for him to go down and meet you,' and to Amanda, 'Tell your brother and sister-in-law that my accountant will come to see them in the next few days.'

Five minutes later Amanda was sitting beside her singing teacher in a taxi on the way to Waterloo Station, and less than half an hour later they were in opposite corners in a crowded railway compartment on the way home. There was no opportunity to talk during the early part of the journey, so Amanda just stared out of the window and reflected on the almost unbelievable fact that the solution to Henry's problem was, as it were, in her pocket.

By the time the train was nearing her station—which was one stop before her companion's—the compartment had more or less cleared and he came to sit beside her. So she summoned her courage to ask, 'May I come to my singing lesson as usual on Sunday?'

'Of course. What else?' he looked surprised. 'You're going to have to work harder than ever if we're to carry out today's tentative plans. There's no opera yet, Amanda. There may never be one. But if there is then you'll be an integral part of it. You get out here, don't you?'

'Yes,' she said. 'But before I go—thank you!' And she leant towards him and kissed him. Then, without waiting to see the effect on him, she opened the door before he could, jumped out of the train and walked rapidly towards the ticket barrier without once looking back.

During the short walk home her thoughts were in such an agitating, exciting state of confusion that nothing seemed to emerge in any coherent form. During the last five or six hours she had experienced some of the worst and some of the best and most vivid moments of her life. But when she walked into the house, to find Nan clearing up on her own in the kitchen, all she could think of saying was, 'It's all right. Henry can go to Switzerland.'

'Mandy!' Nan almost dropped the dish she was holding. Then putting it on a nearby table with visibly shaking hands, she said, 'You mean Arrowsmith gave you a contract?'

'Oh——' Amanda recalled Max Arrowsmith as though he were a figure from an entirely different phase of her life. 'Oh, no, not Max Arrowsmith. It's Oscar Warrender who——'

'*Oscar Warrender*?—gave you a contract?'

'Not exactly. No, of course not.' Amanda made a tremendous effort after coherence. 'He and his wife —and Lewis Elsworth think they may want me for something in the future. And, rather than let me get involved with Arrowsmith, they're prepared to pay for Henry's treatment in Switzerland and for someone to replace him here while he's away.'

'I don't believe it!' Nan paled and looked almost angry. 'You're making it up. Things don't happen like that.'

'I'd have said the same only a few hours ago,' Amanda admitted slowly. 'But it's all perfectly true, Nan. Sit down and I'll try to explain.'

Nan dropped into a chair at one side of the table and Amanda sat down opposite her, rather as they had faced each other on that terrible evening when Nan had had to explain about Henry. Amanda chose her words more carefully now, for she felt it was not yet the moment to tell anyone else about Lewis's composition. That being so, she had to concentrate very much on the idea that Sir Oscar and Lewis wanted to ensure that her vocal training was completed on the lines which they had approved.

'I know it sounds improbable——' she said.

'It sounds totally unbelievable,' retorted Nan, still looking angry because she simply dared not allow herself to accept the reassurance her young sister-in-law was so confidently offering. 'You say Warrender is sending his accountant to see Henry and me?' And then, as Amanda nodded—'But why should he? why should *they* do this extraordinary thing? They must think you're something tremendous, something outstanding that furthers some project of theirs. Men only do things like that for ambition—or love. And I take it Warrender isn't in love with you.'

'Oh, no!' Amanda laughed. 'I don't think he cares the flick of a finger about any woman but his Anthea.'

'Well, that's as may be,' replied Nan in the tone of one who refused to be so credulous about any man of the theatre. 'And what about Lewis Elsworth? Is he in love with you?'

'No, of course not. I'm no more than a particularly promising student so far as he's concerned.'

'You don't say!' Nan looked so ironically amused that Amanda would have demanded to know what she meant if Henry had not come in just then, thus involving her in fresh explanations, though this time with Nan's assistance. Henry also took some convincing that his young sister really had the story right. But then came what Amanda afterwards thought was the most wonderful moment of that wonderful day: when the full truth broke on her brother and he could allow the heavenly relief from pain and anxiety to show for once in his worn face.

To be involved the next morning in the irresistible demands of ordinary routine seemed strange at first, and once or twice Amanda wondered if she really had dreamed some of the events of the previous day. One circumstance registered, however, with unpleasant clarity, and that was the necessity of telephoning Max Arrowsmith and telling him that she was turning down his offer.

Bracing herself for the encounter—and trying to assure herself that she could probably get away with leaving a message with his secretary—she dialled the number which Jerome had once given her. No secretary replied. She was immediately put through to the great man himself and, her throat dry but her tone remarkably cool, she said, 'Mr Arrowsmith, I'm not going to elaborate on things. I just want to tell you that I've thought over your offer and, although I appreciate it, I'm not prepared to accept it.'

'Why not, my dear?'

'Without going into detail—I don't think it's my

kind of work at all, and I don't feel ready to embark on anything professional at this stage. I'm sorry if I'm disappointing you and Jerry—but that is my absolutely final decision.'

'Endorsed by Lewis Elsworth, I take it?'

'You may take it any way you like, Mr Arrowsmith. But that is my last word on it. Thank you and goodbye.'

She was annoyed to find that she was trembling when she replaced the receiver. She was even more annoyed to find that she had not asked him to let Jerome Leydon know her decision. Now she would have to tackle another disagreeable telephone conversation—and she felt ill-prepared to do so. Later, she told herself. She would wait until she had regained her courage and self-control. But each time the telephone bell rang during the next hour she jumped and looked stricken.

Jerome Leydon, however, was not one to conduct important conversations by telephone. He appeared in person early in the afternoon, having timed his visit so that he would have a good chance of getting Amanda to himself. And, taking her gently by the arm, he led her out into the deserted garden behind the hotel, saying, 'Don't look so scared, Mandy. This isn't your dictatorial singing teacher, remember. Just your rather puzzled friend Jerry.'

'Oh, Jerry, I'm so terribly sorry,' she began remorsefully.

'But why, dear? You're perfectly entitled to make your own decisions about anything as important as your career. But I think that in my turn I'm entitled to some sort of explanation, don't you?'

'Yes, yes, of course: and I'll try to explain.' She was so relieved by his easy, almost gentle approach that she could have embraced him. 'Oh, Jerry—' without knowing it she drew a great sigh of relief— 'I thought you'd be absolutely mad with me.'

'Just at first, maybe,' he conceded. 'But even then I was more stunned and puzzled than anything else. I thought you wanted—even *needed*—a lucky break, and I also got the impression that you liked my music. Didn't you care for your song, or the duet we sang together?'

'So far as the music was concerned, I did like it— yes. But as I've told Mr Arrowsmith, I don't think the show as a whole is at all in my line.'

'You didn't wait to hear much of it, did you?' he said ruefully. Amanda wanted to say that she had heard enough *about* it, but remembered just in time that she must not involve Josephine Mead in any way.

'I could make a good guess,' she replied, 'both from what you'd said beforehand and from the words which I had to sing. In addition, I wasn't very favourably impressed by the other people to whom I had to sing.'

He smiled wryly at that and observed drily, 'It was for *you* to impress *them*, my love, not the other way round. But let that pass. You realise you would never —and I mean never—receive another offer from Arrowsmith?'

'I don't want one!'

'And, incidentally, that you brought my stock with him and his backers pretty low? I have been pressing your claims for quite some time.'

'I'm sorry,' she said unhappily.

'But there's no question of your changing your mind?'

'None at all.' She shook her head emphatically.

He sighed slightly at that and then said, 'Mandy, there's one question I want to ask you. Did you in fact discuss the whole thing with Elsworth before making your decision?'

She longed to deny that, but after a tiny pause she admitted, 'Yes, I did. Immediately after I left Mr Arrowsmith's office.'

His eyebrows shot up and he said ironically, 'Don't tell me you just happened to run into him in the street. You must already have arranged to meet him and get his opinion. So you weren't very straight with me when I asked you about him in Arrowsmith's office, were you, Mandy?'

'Oh, I was—I was at the time,' she insisted, and took hold of his arm in her earnestness. 'When I got outside I was totally undecided what to do and then I suddenly thought I would go and—and consult Sir Oscar Warrender. Lewis happened to call while I was there. Neither of them th-thought it was a good idea for me to accept Mr Arrowsmith's offer, so I took their advice.'

'I see.' He sounded suddenly like someone who had come to the end of all argument, and to her utter dismay she realised that, for the first time since she had known him, he looked defeated and depressed.

'Jerry, I wish I hadn't had to upset things so much for you!' In her remorseful distress she ran her hand up and down his arm in a gesture of something between supplication and comfort, and he immediately looked down at her with that charming rueful smile.

'It can't be helped, dear. That's the way things sometimes happen. Only—' he lightly put a hand against her cheek, and the unexpected caress moved her deeply—'this doesn't mean that we can't go on being friends, does it?'

'Of course not!' she cried. 'I'll always be grateful for the support you wanted to give me and the generous way you've accepted my refusal.' She smiled up at him almost tremulously. 'If *you* still feel like being friends it would be pretty shabby of me not to do the same.'

'Seal the pact?' he suggested, and without giving her a chance to reply he bent and kissed her upturned face.

It was perhaps a more deliberate and serious kiss than she would have chosen. But in that emotional moment of renewed friendship she could not have failed to respond, and she kissed him very frankly and sweetly in return. At that his arms went round her and he held her very tightly for a moment or two. Then she gently released herself, turned resolutely towards the house again—and realised that Lewis Elsworth had just stepped out from the French windows and was coming slowly down the path towards them.

CHAPTER SEVEN

JEROME gave a slight whistle of amused dismay as he too became aware of Lewis's approach, while to Amanda the situation seemed to combine all the classic features of a bad dream. There was no possibility of avoiding a disastrous encounter, no hope of explaining away a false impression and no graceful means of eliminating herself from the scene.

Of the three of them only Lewis displayed complete self-possession. As he came up with the other two he nodded casually to Jerome and, addressing himself to Amanda, said, 'Your sister-in-law thought I might find you in the garden, but omitted to mention you already had someone with you.'

'She—she didn't know,' Amanda explained, and then realised that, in her confusion, she had somehow made that sound more significant than it was. 'Jerome was just going anyway,' she added, as though that were some sort of extenuating circumstance. 'Weren't you?'

'If you say so.' His smile at the other man was faintly insolent and his shrug unnecessarily deprecating. Then, perhaps deliberately, he completed an unfortunate impression by saying to Amanda with an air of intimacy, 'We'll finish our talk another time.'

'If I'm interrupting anything vital——' Lewis began. But Amanda said, 'No, no, of course not,' and then wondered if that were the happiest way of dismissing what must have registered as a fond embrace.

130

At that point Jerome took his leave and there was a moment's silence as they both looked after him until he reached the gate. Then Amanda said impulsively, 'I'd like to explain that——'

'Oh, please don't.' Lewis made a slight movement of distaste. 'Nothing is more boring than explanations which don't concern one. I'd better tell you why I'm here.'

'Yes, of course.' She wished she could have sounded less subdued, and even more did she wish she had had the good sense to hold her tongue about the necessity of explaining any action of hers to him. To imply that explanations were due was also to imply that what she did was of personal importance to him. From his expression it was obvious that nothing could be further from the case, and that in fact he was bored by any little flirtation in which she might choose to indulge. So she lapsed into unhappy silence and he went on,

'Patrick Rogerson phoned about an hour ago. Warrender had already got in touch with him and given him some idea of the position. He sounds more than a little interested and wants to come down and see me tomorrow afternoon. I should like you to be there, Amanda. Obviously he'll want to hear something of the music, and to have someone sing it will naturally be more effective than sketching it out on the piano.'

'Of course I'll come!' She could hardly hide her eagerness to please him but hoped he would interpret that as purely artistic interest. 'What time do you need me?'

'About two?' he suggested. 'That would give us time to run through a few things before he arrives and provide some ground for mutual discussion. That basic idea of yours seemed good to me—as though you have some instinct for the whole thing. One could have thought,' he added half to himself, 'that you already *knew* the significance of the setting for that prayer.'

'I'm glad you think I—I might be useful.'

'Of course you can be useful,' he retorted irritably. 'In fact you're essential. Provided—forgive me for making this quite clear—you can manage not to discuss our plans with anyone else, however close they may be to you.'

'I shouldn't dream of it!' she retorted indignantly. 'I had to explain the general position to Nan and my brother—about your all helping Henry, I mean—but I gave as the explanation that you and Sir Oscar wanted to make sure that I completed my training on the right lines. I said nothing whatever about your compositions.'

'I was not thinking primarily of your brother and sister-in-law,' he told her bluntly, at which she flushed and said very curtly,

'If that's a backhanded reference to Jerry Leydon, I also managed to avoid any reference to your work when I was justifying my refusal of Max Arrowsmith's offer.'

'Clever of you in the circumstances,' he conceded, which she found almost insufferably provocative. But this time she managed to resist the longing to justify herself afresh.

Lewis left almost immediately after that and Amanda went slowly into the house, where she found her sister-in-law engaged in dinner preparations. Nan turned to her with interest and said, 'It's the first time I've had anything much to do with your Dr Elsworth. He's nice, isn't he?'

'Sometimes,' replied Amanda equivocally. 'But what makes you say that?'

'He talked quite a bit about Henry and seemed unusually understanding and sympathetic over my anxiety. In fact I don't know whether he ever mentioned this to you?—he said he knew himself the anguish of loving someone who was ill and not being able to do a thing about it.'

'He told you that?' Amanda stared at her sister-in-law in amazement. 'He certainly never told *me* anything so personal in all the time I've known him. You astound me, Nan! How on earth did you get on such a footing?'

'I don't know,' Nan said candidly. 'He was somehow so easy to talk to that I just found myself telling him more about Henry and our problems than I usually would dream of doing with anyone else I can think of. I understand why you're fond of him.'

'I'm not *fond* of him,' Amanda protested quickly. And then, before Nan could query that, 'Who—who was this person he loved and couldn't help?'

'He didn't offer to say.'

'It could have been a brother or sister, I suppose. One of his family anyway,' Amanda said slowly.

'Or someone he would have liked to marry only she died,' Nan suggested. 'Or even—I suppose he never *was* married, was he?'

'Not that I know of.' For some unexplained reason Amanda found the idea both improbable and unacceptable, and she went on quickly, 'He must have been here quite some while before he came out to speak to me in the garden.'

'Oh, not so long,' Nan assured her. 'One can say a lot in a short time if there's immediately a good relationship. We sat in the window there for about ten or fifteen minutes and——'

'Did you face the garden or did he?' asked Amanda sharply.

'He did. Why?' Nan looked surprised.

'It doesn't matter. I—I just wondered how it was you didn't realise I was there.'

'I thought you very well might be, but told him I would check first that you weren't in the house. I left him sitting there in the window, and I suppose he caught sight of you and went out to join you.'

'I suppose he did,' agreed Amanda, accepting with reluctance the certainty that he could not have missed much of the final scene between her and Jerry. 'I was out there with Jerome Leydon, you know. He came about half an hour earlier and we went straight into the garden, so that I could explain about my decision to refuse Max Arrowsmith's offer.'

'And how did he take your refusal?' her sister-in-law asked with interest.

'Beautifully,' replied Amanda almost savagely. 'We ended by pledging renewed friendship and kissing each other.'

'Did you really?' Nan looked amused. 'That isn't much like you.'

'You tell that to Lewis Elsworth! He watched the scene from the window, I gather, and drew all the wrong conclusions.'

'Oh, dear!' Nan laughed, but then she glanced not unkindly at Amanda and added, 'Does that matter, Mandy?'

'No,' said Amanda shortly, 'it doesn't matter in the least.' And she went out of the room, leaving her sister-in-law to look after her thoughtfully.

The next day, just as she was preparing to set out

to cycle to Austin Parva for her appointment with Lewis and Patrick Rogerson, Sir Oscar Warrender's accountant arrived. He proved to be a pleasant, businesslike man who had obviously received such exact instructions with regard to the position that Amanda had no qualms about leaving him to settle everything with her brother and sister-in-law.

Henry seemed surprised at her departure. But, pleading the urgency of her previous arrangement, Amanda determinedly made her escape, already a little anxious about the time she had inevitably lost. Luck was with her and the church clock was striking two as Lewis opened the door in answer to her tug at the brass bell-pull.

He smiled slightly and congratulated her on her punctuality, but very much in the manner of the teacher to his student, and with no trace of the friendly understanding which had seemed to blossom during that afternoon at the Warrenders' flat. Only when they started to go through some of the music he had composed during the last year or so did her enthusiasm and delight add warmth to their exchange of comment and suggestion. By the time Patrick Rogerson arrived Amanda at least felt she was embarked on a thrilling voyage of discovery.

The two men had met before, though only passingly, she gathered, and it seemed to her that they measured each other up with some degree of caution at first. Rogerson greeted Amanda herself with frank interest as he said, 'So you're another of Oscar Warrender's discoveries, are you?'

'No,' Lewis stated firmly, before she could reply for herself. 'She's my discovery.'

'Hh-hm——' Rogerson—a heavily built, good-

looking man in his early forties—glanced amusedly
from one to the other. 'Your discovery and your
inspiration, eh?'

'Oh, no, one couldn't say that!' exclaimed
Amanda, a good deal embarrassed by this description of herself. 'I didn't even know Dr Elsworth
composed until quite recently.'

'But I thought you were the girl that this work is
all about.'

'No, no!' Amanda glanced anxiously in Lewis's
direction and was surprised to see that apparently
he was more amused than affronted. He came to her
rescue at that point.

'Amanda is, I think, peculiarly fitted for the sort of
heroine we all have in mind,' he said mildly. 'Provided of course that a complete work does eventually emerge from the rather fragmentary stuff I have
so far composed.'

'And what,' asked Patrick Rogerson, 'is "the sort
of heroine we all have in mind"?' And he threw himself back in a fragile Queen Anne chair with a degree
of energy that made Amanda wince.

'You'd better explain, Mandy,' said Lewis and,
staggered though she was to hear this informal ver-
sion of her name on his lips, she realised that he was
letting her know that it was up to her to make out a
good case for the work which they both now hoped
to bring to fruition. So once more, with care and
great earnestness, she embarked on a description of
the tentative suggestion she had outlined for the Warrenders. And all the time Patrick Rogerson watched
her, his bold dark eyes intent on her face and the
changing expressions which, without her being aware
of the fact, flitted across her expressive features.

'It's a bit vague,' he said at last. 'Sing me something from it. Warrender said there's an unusual prayer. Uncanny but compelling, was how he described it. He said you made a very telling comment about it.'

'*I* did?' She looked surprised.

'You did,' Lewis confirmed quietly as he went to the piano. 'It's a prayer for warding off the Evil One, and Amanda said the girl sings it when she's learned enough about good to be afraid of evil.'

'Uh-hm. Go on—sing it,' Rogerson ordered her.

So Amanda, with the absolute conviction that this was an important moment, stood beside Lewis and sang it, while Patrick Rogerson sat with his hands lightly clasped between his knees and his gaze on the ground. It disappointed her a little that he did not look at her. But at the end he did look up and said, 'Do you know the words by heart?'

'Almost, I think. They're simple and rather repetitive. Why?'

'Because I want to hear—and see—you do it without the music in your hand. Study the words for a minute or two.'

She went to the window and, standing with her back to the room, concentrated on the words of the prayer. Behind her she was aware of the two men talking quietly to each other. But when she turned and said, 'All right, I think I have it,' they broke off immediately and Rogerson took charge with an air of authority which surprised her.

'Go and stand over there,' he directed her. 'Obviously we have to set the story roughly in the Middle Ages. You've dabbled in witchcraft in the early part —whether through ignorance or intention doesn't matter at the moment. What does matter is that something has happened which has drawn you irresistibly towards the light instead of the dark, but you haven't yet broken completely free. You're now in great danger—in a moment of crisis. Your familiar instinct is to call upon the Evil One but, because of your dawning knowledge, what you pray for is to be saved from him. Now, how would you portray that? Don't hurry. Think about it for a minute or two.'

There was something so compelling about the instructions of this big, forceful man that Amanda tried with all her heart and mind to do what he wanted of her. She stood there for a minute or two just thinking herself into the part he had sketched for her. It was very much how she herself had thought of this strangely beautiful composition of Lewis's, and presently she nodded to Patrick Rogerson and he made a slight gesture of his hand to Lewis who immediately played the opening phrases.

In the most extraordinary way it seemed to Amanda that the familiar room began to change subtly, the light faded, and she was alone and very much afraid. The simple words, the strangely beautiful music were both there, ready to express exactly how she was feeling. Not a thing did she need to invent. It was as though she had known this scene all her life. And when she had sung the last notes she found she was on her knees and crying.

'You're a fortunate man,' she heard Patrick Rogerson say. 'The girl is a natural artist.'

'I know,' Lewis replied. Then he came across, picked her up off the floor and said, 'Don't cry, Mandy,' and kissed her.

'I'm sorry, I didn't mean to be so silly.' She was divided between shamed surprise at her own emotion and astonishment that Lewis should have kissed her

and once more addressed her by that half affectionate shortening of her name.

'What stage experience have you had?' Rogerson
wanted to know.

'None,' Amanda told him.

'None?' He sounded curiously satisfied. 'She's a
natural, I tell you,' he remarked again to Lewis.
'She'll need a certain amount of basic professional
stage training, of course. Maybe Warrender might
find her a place in the chorus, or a small walk-on part
or something of the kind. Just to give her the feel of
the stage. We'll discuss it. And now to go back to
your work, Elsworth——' he grinned at Lewis in a
friendly way. 'Is that the one and only flash of genius
or——?'

'Oh, no!' It was Amanda who replied with determination this time. 'There's a lot more lovely stuff.
You must hear some of it. Dr Elsworth can make
shift to sing tenor or baritone.'

'All right.' Patrick Rogerson gave her an indulgent
glance. 'And I daresay I can supply a bit of bass
growling if necessary.'

There followed what was to Amanda one of the
most exciting experiences of her life. There was no
question about Rogerson's interest and approval. He
sang, Lewis sang and Amanda sang, all of them
breaking off from time to time while Rogerson threw
in a suggestion about a dramatic possibility or something to do with basic construction—only to with-
draw it ten minutes later in favour of a re-alignment
of plot or a flash of fresh inspiration.

'It's the oddest way to construct a theatrical piece,'
he said at last with a laugh, 'and of course there's a
great deal of grinding desk work to be done. But I'll
stick my neck out here and now and say that I think

we've got something pretty good, even if it's only in the making at the moment. Maybe I'm over-enthusiastic—' he frowned passingly at the possibility—'but it's a heady experience to find a lovely singer and a gifted composer all in one afternoon.'

'Where do we go from here?' Amanda asked breathlessly. 'I mean, we can't waste time just exulting over it.'

'She's a girl after my own heart,' Rogerson told Lewis, again with that infectious grin. ' "At once" is hardly soon enough for her! Well, Miss Amanda, if Elsworth has time to spare—'

'For this, yes,' Lewis put in quickly.

'—I think I'd better find somewhere to stay in the neighbourhood during the next month or two, and we'll get to work right away.'

'You could stay at our hotel, The Nightingale,' Amanda said shyly. 'It's small but it's very comfortable and my sister-in-law cooks like an angel. It isn't more than three miles away. I cycle over twice a week. But if you have a car of course it wouldn't be more than ten or twelve minutes' run.'

'Well, that seems to settle my part of the problem,' Patrick Rogerson agreed. 'All you have to do—' he smiled at Lewis as though he already welcomed him as an artistic partner—'is to go on composing for all you're worth, but now on the basis of setting to music what I write for the libretto. As for you, Miss Amanda, we'll see what Warrender has in mind in the way of stage experience.'

Amanda looked startled, but enjoyably so. 'Do you mean that I might have to go to London and stay there?'

'If Warrender said so,' Rogerson assured her. 'Unless you have someone around here who drives to

London fairly regularly and would give you a lift. Is there anyone in your circle who might fill the bill?'

For a pregnant moment Amanda and Lewis irresistibly exchanged a glance, then she said steadily, 'I'm afraid I don't know anyone like that.'

'Well, the train service is reasonably good, I believe,' Rogerson shrugged. 'No real problem about that.'

'Except that Amanda will still require her twice-weekly singing lesson,' stated Lewis firmly. 'And she also has family demands on her time.'

'In the circumstances I'm sure Nan would manage to dispense with me for a while and get casual village help,' Amanda offered eagerly.

'And as for singing lessons,' added Rogerson with what seemed to Amanda magnificent casualness, 'it's not impossible that Warrender might offer to do something. I presume you would both accept him as a suitable stand-in for the odd singing lesson?' Then he laughed a good deal at Amanda's expression and asked not unkindly, 'Are you scared of him? Most singers are, I know.'

'Not exactly—scared,' said Amanda, not quite truthfully. 'I just thought it highly unlikely that he would even dream of giving singing lessons to a complete beginner, professionally speaking.'

'You'd be surprised,' Rogerson told her seriously. 'There are few things he's not prepared to do if his interest is fully aroused.'

'And you think his interest is fully aroused?' Amanda caught her breath.

'I don't think there's any doubt about it,' Rogerson said. 'Whether it's you or the work or a combination of the two—which is the most likely—I couldn't say. But when I talked with him yesterday he was like a gold prospector who's turned up some grains of gold and expects a pretty sizeable nugget to follow.'

Both Amanda and Lewis laughed at this graphic description, though Lewis said sceptically, 'On the strength of one aria extremely well sung?'

'Oh, no! Not even Warrender would follow a hunch on so little. But I understand he's heard Amanda on another occasion and has seen quite a lot of your stuff in manuscript, besides being impressed by what was said when you all first discussed the project.'

'Objection withdrawn,' conceded Lewis with a smile. 'Your optimism is extraordinarily infectious, Rogerson. From now on I expect difficulties to melt away with dramatic completeness.'

And that, thought Amanda during the next week or two, was very much what happened. First there was the almost incredible ease with which the arrangements were made for Henry's departure for Switzerland, aided by the fact that it was Lewis who surprisingly found an excellent substitute for him while he was away.

'John Partington was an old friend of my father and I've known him most of my life,' he explained. 'He's a retired accountant with a little specialised knowledge of the hotel business as he did about a year in that line just after he retired. He has recently lost his wife and would be very willing to take on a temporary job of this kind.'

'What sort of age, if he's retired?' enquired Nan briskly.

'Late sixties. But very energetic and totally reliable. A likeable man,' said Lewis. And on further acquaintance and during his few days of discussion with Henry over the transfer of duties and records, he proved to be all that Lewis had claimed.

'You say he was a friend of your father,' Amanda remarked when she was discussing the appointment at her next singing lesson. 'It's the first time I've heard you mention your family. Are your parents still alive?'

'No.' He shook his head. 'They were both killed in a plane crash, coming home from the States.'

'*Both* of them? What a tragedy for you!'

'But not perhaps for them,' he said reflectively. 'They were so completely devoted to each other that I can't really imagine either going on even relatively happily without the other. That wasn't the way I saw it at the time, of course, being only seventeen and with a younger sister to look after.'

She thought suddenly what a nice elder brother he must have been, and then enquired quite naturally about his sister now.

'Five years ago she married a Canadian doctor with whom she's tremendously happy', he smiled as though that reflection gave him great pleasure. 'They have two children and live in Montreal.'

Remembering what Nan had told her, Amanda would have liked to enquire further, but he evidently considered they had discussed his personal affairs sufficiently and went on with the lesson. Afterwards, however, she reflected that, short though the conversation had been, it had supplied the answer to most of the questions posed by his conversation with Nan. Whoever it was that he had loved and mourned, it was no one in his own family—a circumstance which was of course nothing to do with her at all, but one which still prompted a certain amount of dissatisfied speculation.

John Partington was not the only one to be in-

stalled at The Nightingale with remarkable speed and
smoothness. Within a matter of days Patrick Rogerson had also taken up his quarters there and, with his
unique blend of cheerful good humour and unusually subtle understanding of people, he made himself
immediately popular, not only with the Lovetts but
with everyone who came to the hotel.

It was he who softened the harsh ordeal of Henry's
departure. For the fact was that, however happy Nan
and Amanda might be in the knowledge that his
trip to Switzerland would very possibly restore his
health, they both knew that they would miss him
sorely. Fortunately young Clive was due home for
the school holidays in a week or two's time so that
Nan at least would have someone to take up her time
and rejoice her heart.

For Amanda life went on in a familiar pattern at
first. She was extra busy helping Nan, her singing
lessons required more intensive study than ever, but
in addition she found herself included in some of
the not always peaceful discussions which took place
between Lewis and Patrick Rogerson.

Both of them, Amanda discovered with amused interest, displayed more than a hint of what is usually
known as 'artistic temperament' and both, involved
as they were in the strain and excitement of creation,
were sometimes short-tempered and impatient with
each other—and with her.

She took it all in good part usually, regarding it as
her contribution to the success of the joint venture.
But one day when she had expended a lot of energy
in bringing peace into a stormy discussion, she said
with a sigh, 'It's a bit wearing being a buffer state
between you two.'

'You're not a buffer state,' Rogerson told her with a grin. 'You're more of a lightning conductor. A soothing influence, that's what you are. I can feel the irritation and unreason oozing out of me when you smile persuasively and make tactful and pacific remarks. How about you, Lewis?'

'How about me in what way?' Lewis asked absently, without even looking up from the page of manuscript he was altering.

'Weren't you listening at all? I was talking about Amanda and asking how you feel about her.'

'How *I* feel——?' He did glance up then and for the first time she could remember Amanda saw him look extremely startled. Then Rogerson laughed and said,

'Merely a surface judgment, old boy. I was praising her for the way she calms down our artistic blow-ups, and I give her full marks as a lightning conductor when we're both letting off sparks and flashes. How about you?'

'She knows what I think about her,' replied Lewis, and went on with his work. And that was the moment when it came to Amanda that she did *not* really know what he thought about her and that it was the most important unanswered question in her whole existence.

The discovery shook her and she was rather silent during the rest of the session. She was even unusually uncommunicative on the short drive home with Patrick Rogerson, and presently he glanced at her and said, 'You're very quiet. You weren't really troubled about that set-to between us this afternoon, were you? It doesn't mean anything when Lewis and I go for each other. Or only that we both think so well of this enterprise that we're ready to fight any-one—even each other—for what we think will be best.'

'Oh, no, of course not! I accept that as part of your joint creation. Only you tease him too much sometimes, Patrick. He's touchy about personal things. You really startled him—didn't you notice? —when you asked what he thought of me.'

'Did I?' Rogerson looked amused. 'Why? Is it a delicate subject?' And when she made a movement of protest he went on before she could speak, 'You mean he's sweet on you and didn't want the fact commented on?'

'I don't mean that at all,' she retorted with emphasis.

'No? Well, it could prove true all the same, I suppose. It would be difficult to work with a darling like you and not be a little sweet on you,' he declared, but with an air of careless good nature which reduced the issue to a reassuringly unimportant level.

Even so, Amanda was still very thoughtful when they arrived home and Nan came out to greet them with unusual eagerness, as though she could not wait for them to enter the house.

'Hello, Nan! News from Switzerland?' enquired Amanda quickly.

'No. It's a bit too early for that yet. But news from London,' replied her sister-in-law with an excited little laugh. 'Lady Warrender phoned while you were out. It's been arranged for you to have classes at his opera school—Sir Oscar's, I mean. And he'll probably give you some intensive training himself. You're to be in London by the beginning of next week, and will be staying there, except for weekends, for the next month or two.'

'Staying there?' gasped Amanda. 'Staying where, for heaven's sake? It isn't too easy to find a cheap place in London, though I suppose I could——'

'That's the cream of the message,' Nan informed her. 'You're to stay with them—the Warrenders. It was Lady Warrender's idea and he's agreed to it. How's that for news?'

CHAPTER EIGHT

'Your basic training has been excellent.' Oscar Warrender got up from the piano and indicated to Amanda that she should sit on the sofa beside his wife. 'Elsworth is obviously a good teacher and you appear to have been a reasonably intelligent pupil. But these are no more than the minimum requirements for the creation of a worthwhile performer, you understand.'

'Dr Elsworth did impress that on me,' Amanda replied submissively. For although she had now been three days in the Warrender household this was the first time the great man had given her a formal hearing and she was still considerably in awe of him.

'At this stage,' Warrender went on, 'you are in the same category as a pianist who has been presented with a fine, well-tuned piano and has developed a good technique. From that point everything depends on what you do with those two essentials. How much artistry, instinct, intelligence and sheer hard work you are capable of bringing to bear on the problem of developing what's within *you*—the unique you which distinguishes you from everyone else. Do you follow me?'

Amanda nodded and looked expectant.

'You show some signs of innate artistry and a natural sense of drama. Many performers who make quite good careers go no further than that, and indeed in this age of monumental mediocrity that's often all that is asked of them. But——'

He paused and Amanda, unable to restrain her eagerness to hear more, said impulsively, 'You mean there's something else which distinguishes the real artist? Something that I—I just possibly might have?'

'Difficult to tell at this early stage, but—' he glanced at his wife—'what would you say, Anthea?'

'Are you talking of star quality?' Anthea enquired.

'Not precisely—no. Nothing so immediately arresting as that. But there is an occasional flash of something totally individual. Don't take that as a compliment, Amanda, or start preening yourself. I'm merely considering vague possibilities, none of which will come to fruition without untiring co-operation on your part. Remember that.'

'I'll remember,' Amanda promised gravely. 'You mean that whatever I have within me is a sort of trust and can only be brought out by my own work and dedication.'

'Something like that.' The conductor smiled slightly.

'Dr Elsworth told me much the same thing. But—' she hesitated and then went on diffidently —'he never spoke of any unique quality. Could you perhaps explain a little more about that?'

'I'll try.' He frowned consideringly. 'I would say it's the ability to give the breath of life to a character who otherwise exists only on paper. So much so that an intelligent member of the audience will be impelled to wonder what happened to that character after the performance is over.'

Anthea laughed, but in obvious agreement, and Amanda, catching her breath slightly, said, 'And you think I just might have that quality?'

'I thought you showed a hint of it when you were

here that afternoon with Elsworth. That's why I was determined to have the handling of you myself,' replied Warrender coolly.

'But I'm not aware of consciously striving after anything like that,' Amanda protested anxiously.

'No, of course not. I'm inclined to think it's a quality one can neither teach nor learn. We'll see—we'll see.' He glanced at his watch. 'I must go now. I have a rehearsal.' And he went before Amanda could ask any more. Before, in fact, she could even express her appreciation of his interest and advice.

'I ought to have thanked him!' she exclaimed remorsefully to Anthea as she heard the front door close. 'I was so—so awed I couldn't think of anything to say. Even now I find it hard to believe that anyone so famous and knowledgeable should take such a kind interest in me. Will you please tell him how truly grateful I am?'

'Yes, I'll tell him,' Anthea promised with a smile. 'But kindness is not what's prompting him, you know. Don't think all this is going to be made easy, Amanda, or that there'll be any preferential treatment for you just because he's taking a hand in your training. He's a very hard taskmaster indeed, and no one knows it better than I do. I also was his pupil.'

'I had heard as much,' Amanda replied, and she looked at Anthea Warrender with a sort of shy curiosity. 'Was he *very* hard on you?'

'Perfectly horrible,' replied Anthea cheerfully. 'I hated the sight of him half the time. But I realised from the first that he was a genius and that I was lucky to be bullied by him. Even when I pretty well wanted him to drop dead in front of me I was still aware that he was the only person who could give me unshakeable confidence when he was at the conductor's desk. It's all a long time ago——' she broke off and laughed reminiscently.

'How long ago?' asked Amanda.

'Since I first sang under him?'

'Since you first met him.'

'O—oh—' Anthea laughed again—'that was a disaster! It was during a singing contest in my home town and he was one of the judges. I desperately needed the big money prize offered because things were difficult at home and I knew that I couldn't continue my training without money from *some-* where. I thought—and I still think, Amanda—that I was the best of the contestants. Most of the judges thought so too, but Oscar talked them over and the prize went to another girl, who was awfully good in her own way, I must admit,' she added fairly.

'But didn't he think you were the best?'

'Oh, yes, he knew I was. But he was determined to save me from a bit of cheap early success and the sort of publicity which would have put me on the wrong path from the beginning. So he did me out of the prize, and then arranged through someone else that I should be sent to him for lessons.'

'That was pretty ruthless, surely?' Amanda looked slightly shocked.

'But they *are* ruthless, Amanda, these men who live for their art and have contempt for anything or anyone who stands in the way of the standards they serve. The maddening thing is of course that they're almost invariably right. Always in Oscar's case, so far as I know,' she added with shameless partiality, 'and probably nearly always in the case of your Lewis Elsworpe. I suppose that's why we start by hating them and end by loving them,' she added half to herself. 'At least, that was how it was with me,' she amended hastily as she saw the startled expression which came over Amanda's face.

'When did you begin to feel differently towards Sir Oscar?' asked Amanda, refusing to particularise about her own affairs.

'Oh, Amanda, I don't quite know. I realised I was in love with him the first night he conducted for me, when I sang Desdemona. But I suppose if I hadn't been so mad with him for other things I'd have recognised the fact sooner.'

'And he?' Amanda could not resist enquiring. 'Was he equally vague about when it happened to him?'

'No, no. Most unkindly exact, I remember. After that Desdemona performance he told me that he'd fallen in love with my voice the first time he heard it. But by then I wanted to hear that he loved *me* and I asked him outright if it had only been my voice he fell instantly in love with—and he said it was.'

'Oh!' Amanda's exclamation of shocked sympathy made the other girl laugh.

'Just how I felt at that moment,' she admitted, 'and, because I was tense and excited after the performance, I began to cry. Then he said it had taken him two and a half weeks to fall in love with me myself—and I could have hit him.' She smilingly shook her head and added, again in that reminiscent tone of voice, 'It's all years ago—nearly twelve years ago, now I come to think of it—but I can remember it as though it were yesterday. How did we come to talk about this, for goodness' sake?'

'We were talking about the ruthlessness of the dedicated artist and—and the fact that one tends to forgive them and love them all the same,' Amanda said slowly.

'Yes, I remember now. Don't worry, my dear. I was generalising. Just concentrate on working the way Oscar directs you. That will give you plenty to think about for the moment.'

Recognising this for good and kindly advice, Amanda tried to follow it during the ensuing weeks and found how exactly Anthea had estimated her husband's handling of a pupil. It was true that he was ruthless, even brutal occasionally in a cold way, but absolutely tireless in his quest for perfection; and his very few words of praise—though gained at the expense of much anguish—were something to be treasured.

He had no personal part in her day-to-day lessons at the school, but here Amanda found she was comfortably abreast of her fellow students as she absorbed the basic technique of stage performance. At a later point she was allowed some chorus work and a walk-on part so small that it comprised little more than a couple of lines. But to each task she devoted the utmost care and attention, gaining a nod of approval from Warrender when he discovered that she had familiarised herself with the complete work even before she set foot on the stage at rehearsal for her two lines.

Meanwhile the news from home was good. Most of this came by letter from Nan, who proved to be an unusually good correspondent, and occasionally—though more occasionally than she had expected—she was able to go back to The Nightingale for an odd weekend.

'I thought,' Nan said to her on the occasion of one of her rare visits, 'that the idea was for you to come home most weekends.'

'I thought so too,' Amanda agreed. 'But that

doesn't seem to be Sir Oscar's idea. He sets my time-table and I couldn't even imagine querying it. He's terribly strict.'

'But nice on the whole, I take it?'

'Nice? Oh, no, you couldn't describe Oscar War-render as *nice*, any more than you could describe Niagara Falls or Mount Everest as nice. He's tremen-dously stimulating and inspiring and a genius and all that. But if you have anything to do with him pro-fessionally he takes over your life and, in a curious way, you're thrilled to have him do so. That may sound silly, but it's true.'

'Well, I don't complain of the way he's partly taken over *our* lives either,' Nan replied with a laugh, and Amanda realised suddenly that her sister-in-law looked unusually happy and oddly reminiscent of the lovely girl who had married Henry. 'I had the latest news from Dr Charole this morning. He's cautious, of course—he always is—and I hardly dare to hope too much, but it's much the best report yet.'

'Let me see!' cried Amanda, and when she too had read the doctor's account of Henry's progress since his operation, she hugged Nan and exclaimed, 'It's going to be all right. I *know* it's going to be all right. Blessings on the Warrenders! And on Lewis too, of course,' she added a little awkwardly.

'And Lewis too,' Nan echoed with a smile. 'He and Patrick have been in and out most days this week, enquiring about you. It seems they've reached some point where they need you.—And, talking of angels (if that's the right description for them), here they are, I think.'

Two minutes later both Lewis and Patrick Roger-son came in.

'Here's our girl at last!' exclaimed Rogerson, kissing Amanda with a sort of casual heartiness which was in marked contrast to the slight smile with which Lewis greeted her. 'We thought Warrender had decided to take you over for some scheme of his own,' Rogerson went on, 'and that you proposed to desert us and our work.'

'*I* never thought that,' stated Lewis calmly.

'I should hope not indeed!' exclaimed Amanda. 'After all you've done for me? Why, your claims come before anything Sir Oscar or anyone else could suggest. *Nothing* could ever make me forget our family debt to you,' she ended passionately.

'Well, forget it now,' Lewis told her curtly, and she had the odd impression that what she had said did not please him. Nan also was evidently aware of his reaction because she put her hand on his arm, with an easy familiarity which Amanda envied, and said, 'Don't look so cross and self-conscious. *You* can forget if you like, but we never can.'

'Oh, please——' he frowned and made a quick movement of rejection, while his companion looked amused and curious.

'All right, I won't labour the point,' Nan conceded. 'But we've just had wonderful news from Switzerland and we naturally associate it with you and the Warrenders.'

'May one ask——' began Rogerson.

'No, one may not,' Lewis interrupted shortly. 'It's not important anyway. What is important is that we can take Amanda back with us and put her through a vital scene in the second act. We've worked on it until we can hardly be civil to each other, Amanda, and we have to hear you sing it and give us some idea of what it's like when delivered in person. It needs what one might call the breath of life to lift it

from the manuscript page and make a real thing of it.
—Why do you look like that?' he added curiously.

'Because of what you said,' Amanda replied. 'You
used almost exactly the same term as Sir Oscar when
he——'

'When he what?' Lewis looked at her intently.

'When he auditioned me formally for the first time
he—he said I just might have the unusual quality
which enables an artist to give the breath of life to
a character who exists otherwise only on paper.'

'So he recognised it too!' Lewis put out his hand
and, as though Nan and Rogerson were not there, he
drew her against him and looked down at her.

'He thought I showed a hint of it when I sang that
prayer in the last act. And I thought how wonderful
it would be if I could help to give life to a character
created by you.'

'If you succeed in that don't ever again speak of
being in debt to me,' he said with a slight smile, and
he bent his head and kissed her cheek. It was a much
lighter kiss than the exuberant salute Patrick Rogerson had bestowed upon her, but to Amanda it conveyed more than any other kiss she had ever received.

She thought that surely Nan and Patrick Rogerson
must have noted the significance of the moment. But
when she looked up they were discussing the all-
important report from Switzerland, and Amanda
wondered confusedly if she had read more into that
kiss than was intended.

'Well——' Lewis spoke quite briskly this time—
'we're going to snatch Amanda away now. We'll
leave her free tomorrow, so that's a fair division.'

'As she likes,' Nan smiled. 'But be back before ten,
Mandy. I forgot to tell you—Jeremy has phoned two
or three times in the last few days and yesterday I

told him you'd be home this weekend and suggested he phone about ten this evening.'

Only when Lewis abruptly dropped her hand did Amanda realise that he had continued to hold it. But before she could make any comment Patrick Rogerson said easily, 'I'll undertake to have her home in time for the vital call. So you know Jerry Leydon, do you?—Attractive fellow. Very talented too.'

No one seemed to have anything to add to this, and Amanda went out to the car with a talkative Patrick Rogerson and a silent Lewis.

But no touch of embarrassment or strain could cloud the hours which followed. She was astounded and thrilled to discover how much work had been accomplished during the weeks she had been away. When she voiced her amazement, however, Lewis explained that there had been a considerable volume of music already written and only a certain amount of adaptation and rearrangement had been necessary for the first and third acts.

'Patrick was remakably skilful over that,' he conceded generously.

'That's right,' agreed Rogerson brazenly. 'But then it's my kind of work, and the sense of excitement and adventure kept one at it. Some nights I hardly went to bed. There's some wonderful stuff for the two men as well as for you, Amanda.'

'Don't be so confident that it's specifically for me,' exclaimed Amanda, crossing her fingers. 'Remember that the actual casting lies with the conductor and producer. Neither of them may want to trust it to a total beginner when it comes to the point.'

'Has Warrender hinted as much?' asked Lewis quickly.

'No. It's never been discussed on a practical basis,

but the facts speak for themselves, don't they? If the work turns out to be as fine as we all hope then no conscientious conductor—least of all Sir Oscar—would dream of weakening it by wrong casting.'

'The part is your part,' stated Lewis, setting his mouth in an obstinate line. 'It waits for performance until you're ready to play it.'

'I'm afraid Sir Oscar would say that any work of quality is more important than any performer. And he would be right,' Amanda said, but she gave him a brilliant smile. 'I'll do my best; of course I'll do my best. But we're talking about lovely possibilities at too early a stage.' And suddenly she felt the burden of a tremendous responsibility weighing upon her.

'Well, let's finish the work,' interjected Rogerson cheerfully, 'and argue about the casting afterwards. We haven't got the second act as we want it yet.'

'Musically I've almost got it,' muttered Lewis. 'I only needed to hear Amanda sing that early passage. But now the mood changes too rapidly, which leaves us not enough conflict for the last act. If we strengthen this here——' He and Rogerson hung over the sheets of manuscript together while Amanda sat and watched them, allowing her mind to wander over the extraordinary possibilities which these two men were weaving.—For her? or for someone else?

It was difficult to realise, even now, that this was all anything more than an exciting piece of make-believe.

'I don't *feel* that I shall ever be on a stage, singing and acting what they are at this very moment creating,' she thought. 'Have I got a spark of the divine fire which makes an artist? Have I even got the competitive spirit which takes people to the top? At the moment all that I desperately want is that Lewis's work should succeed. I'd rather someone else made a success of it than that I did it less than justice. That's terribly unambitious of me, I suppose. But then I'm not madly ambitious. I just *know* how that girl in the opera thinks and acts and ticks. As though she's trying to push me into representing her and making her real. If I get the chance——'

'Come here, Amanda,' said Lewis at that moment, and she went to him immediately and listened intently while he explained the short scene on which he and Rogerson had been engaged. 'What would she do in those circumstances?' he asked abruptly.

'What would she do?' Amanda repeated slowly. 'You mean what would *I* do?'

Rogerson made as though to speak, but Lewis silenced him with a peremptory gesture and said softly, 'All right. What would you do? She *is* you in a way. Passionate inside and yet sufficiently unawakened to be passive in the grasp of events. This is the moment when reality begins to break in on her. How would you show it?'

'Mostly in movement at first,' Amanda said, still speaking slowly, and she began to pace round the room without much sense of direction, like a graceful animal seeking to find a lost track. Then she stopped and muttered something and Lewis, sitting at the piano, provided a few hesitant chords at which she nodded. She began to pace again and the phrases became more coherent, but repetitive as though she were impressing something on her own consciousness. Then suddenly she stopped and threw out her arms and instantly he launched into the strong, positive air which he had made her sing earlier in the afternoon.

'Something like that,' said Amanda, as though suddenly coming to herself again.

'Yes, something like that,' Lewis agreed in a deeply satisfied tone of voice. While Rogerson, staring from one to the other, said,

'You two give me the willies! Is this an act or something? I'd have said you were hypnotising her if I hadn't known you too well for that. How did you know what to do, Amanda?'

'I didn't—I was just suggesting what I think she would do. That was what you asked for, wasn't it, Lewis?'

'Yes. It's a case of two minds being very much in tune,' he explained briefly to Rogerson. 'Thank you, Amanda. I'll work on it that way and see if we were right.'

'Well, I suppose you know what you're doing.' The other man looked half amused, half protesting. 'But you made the hair stand up at the back of my neck! How about the wording required for that bit where she's wandering around?'

'Very simple. Repetitive at first, positive and coherent when she suddenly sees the way. I'll give you the clues when I've worked on it. It's the last real problem, I think.' He smiled and the colour flushed up in his face. 'After that there's only some tidying up and extra scoring—and we're almost home.'

'"Only!"' repeated Rogerson with good-humoured scorn. 'Quite a tough assignment still. However, time is on our side. Apart from bringing our Amanda up to scratch for the great task, we may still have to wait God knows how long for the chance of seeing it actually performed.'

'Of course.' Lewis suddenly stifled a yawn and his voice sounded almost languid. 'Take Amanda home —she's probably nearly as whacked as I am. And I suppose even you are feeling the strain by now.'

'Do you need either of us tomorrow?' Amanda asked.

'No, no.' Lewis shook his head almost impatiently. 'I must work on this myself to get it right. You're going back to London tomorrow evening, I take it? Give my greetings to the Warrenders and tell him——' he stopped suddenly and then frowned and said, 'No, don't tell him anything. I may not have it right even now.'

'You're sure you won't need me tomorrow?' She tried to make that casual, but was dismayed to find that it came out with a touch of wistfulness, and she felt humiliated when he replied absently, 'Quite sure. Go along now. Nan said something about wanting you home before ten, didn't she?'

Stung by his absentminded dismissal of her, tired after the intense concentration of the last few hours, she had an impulse to sting him in return. 'That's right,' she replied deliberately. 'Nan said Jerry would be phoning, and I shouldn't like to miss him. Goodnight.'

She then walked out of the room ahead of Patrick Rogerson, and was already ensconced in the car when, having exchanged a few last words with Lewis, he came out to join her.

'Jerome Leydon doesn't seem to be much of a favourite with Lewis,' he remarked as he started the car. Then, as she made no reply to that, 'Is Lewis jealous of him?'

'I shouldn't think so. Their paths don't cross professionally, do they?' replied Amanda, with an admirable assumption of indifference.

'I didn't mean professionally. I thought it had something to do with you.'

'Oh—' she produced a careless little laugh with some success—'that isn't jealousy. Didn't you know? He was angry because Jerry introduced me to Max Arrowsmith, who made me an offer to sing in one of his shows. Lewis wouldn't hear of it, and nor would Sir Oscar. So I turned it down, of course.'

'But still remained friendly with Leydon?' Rogerson glanced at her curiously.

'Why not?' Amanda shrugged. 'His interest was a genuinely friendly one, and he didn't hold it against me that I refused Arrowsmith's offer.'

'Are you sure he didn't?'

'Quite sure,' said Amanda, and immediately wondered if that were the exact truth. 'Why do you ask?'

'Only that he must be more forgiving than I would have supposed if he was willing to have his discovery filched from him just as he'd got her to the point of interesting Arrowsmith.'

'There was no *filching* about it,' she retorted angrily. 'And it would be exaggerating to say that he was exactly willing to lose me to someone else. He bowed more or less gracefully to the inevitable. He just had to, really. That's show business, isn't it?' she added, feeling that this comment sounded rather chic and professional.

'It is, my dear,' Rogerson agreed goodhumouredly as they drove up to The Nightingale. 'And a pretty harsh and cut-throat business it is too, if I may say so. My guess is that Leydon—and certainly Arrowsmith—would be happy to hand round a poisoned loving-cup to Lewis and you—and Warrender too, I imagine. It's a good thing we don't all live in the time of the Borgias.'

'Oh, hush!' exclaimed Amanda warningly, for as they stopped before the door she saw that Jerome

Leydon was standing there, smiling a welcome.

She jumped out of the car almost before it had stopped and ran to greet him, aware of the most extraordinary pleasure in the unexpected appearance of someone who didn't criticise her or brush her off when he was busy; who, on the contrary, cherished no ill-will even when she had rejected the help he wanted to offer.

He laughed delightedly at her eagerness, almost lifted her off her feet and kissed her.

'I thought you were going to phone,' she said breathlessly, and turned to introduce Rogerson, only to find that he had already driven off towards the garage.

'A visit seemed a better idea,' Jerome explained 'What time tomorrow have you available for an old friend?'

'Oh, Jerry, I must spend some time with Nan. I've hardly seen anything of her. I had—' she swallowed—'a very long singing session this afternoon. And I'm going back to London tomorrow evening.'

'Then I'll drive you,' he offered. And, in spite of a faint unexplained flutter of disquiet, she said that would be a wonderful idea.

'Are you coming in now?' she gestured towards the house.

'No. I've had half an hour's chat with Nan. And I really only came to say hello and pin you down to some sort of meeting tomorrow before rival claims were put in. How are things going for you, Mandy?'

'Pretty well. It's hard work, but rewarding, having Sir Oscar direct my studies.'

'I can believe it. Which reminds me——' he smiled, and she would have said there was a touch of malice in his smile if she had not known how good-natured he was. 'Friend Warrender will have taken a bit of a knock over this Northern Counties Festival disaster.'

'What disaster?' she asked quickly. 'I understood everything was going splendidly.'

'I suppose it was,' he said indifferently, 'until Julian Tankerton had this bad car crash. Perhaps you hadn't heard? It only happened today. He obviously won't be able to complete that opera of his which was to have been the highlight of Warrender's precious Festival. Pity,' he added cheerfully.

'Is he badly hurt?'

'He'll recover, but it will take a long time—too long for his work to be used this year. Ah well, Warrender can do with a bit of chastening. He does rather think he's God Almighty, doesn't he?'

'No, he does not,' Amanda retorted coldly, and she withdrew the hand which Jerome had tucked into the crook of his elbow. 'Anyway, I'm sure he'll be able to come up with a good alternative.'

'Not altogether easy, Mandy. People are used to Warrender producing a thoroughly worthwhile novelty at any festival he promotes. Either a work or an artist—or both. I rather look forward to seeing the critics hint that he's losing his touch.'

'I think I'll go in now,' said Amanda curtly. 'I'm tired. I'll see you tomorrow. Would it suit you to fetch me about six-thirty?'

'It would indeed.' He smiled at her, but she did not smile back. She merely said, 'Otherwise I can quite easily take the train.'

'You will not take the train, my love. You will give me the pleasure of driving you,' he told her, laughing. 'And you needn't look so cross with me just because I offered the mildest criticism of your

Sir Oscar. There are lots of people who hate his guts. I only dislike him—and mildly wish him ill. Oh, Mandy, don't be silly!' as she almost pettishly turned away. 'I'm only teasing you. Come on, kiss me and say it's all right.'

So Amanda kissed him and said it was all right. Not because she felt any more friendly disposed towards him, but because the most tremendous excitement was growing within her and she hardly saw how she could keep it from him much longer. Was it remotely possible that a substitute—the substitute— might be found to replace poor Julian Tankerton's work? It was hard to tell when one knew so little about how long it took to complete a work on paper and then put it on to a stage.

She bade Jerome goodnight and went indoors. She contrived to answer Nan's queries about her afternoon's work and to gossip idly of family affairs and prospects. She even managed to give a convincing yawn or two before going upstairs to bed. But after that her excited thoughts and hopes took over and she lay awake until the first streaks of dawnlight were in the sky.

In consequence she was rather heavy-eyed when she came down to breakfast, but she succeeded in sounding almost casual as she informed Nan that she had to cycle over to Austin Parva that afternoon.

'I realise there are still one or two points I need to discuss with Lewis before going back to London,' she asserted.

'But why drag over there by bike?' Nan wanted to know. 'You look tired enough already. I'm sure Patrick would run you over.'

'No, no, I don't want to tell—I don't want to impose on him,' she corrected herself quickly. 'Anyway, I'd *like* a cycle ride,' she insisted, and there was an almost fretful note in her voice which made Nan raise her eyebrows and say, 'Please yourself.'

It was all she could do to contain her impatience until the afternoon, when she knew Lewis would be free from his Sunday duties at the church. But when at last she was on her bicycle, speeding towards Austin Parva, the tension relaxed so sharply that her spirits suddenly dropped to zero, and she told herself that she was going on a fool's errand. She had just been indulging in the sort of extravagant hopes and dreams which characterised the totally inexperienced person.

At that point she almost turned back. But a tiny flame of illogical hope still kept her going, and when she turned into the familiar main street and came within sight of the small white-painted house where Lewis lived, the flame shot up to unbelievable heights. For standing in front of Lewis's house was an unmistakable car. The long black Daimler of Oscar Warrender.

CHAPTER NINE

WHEN Lewis opened the door in answer to her agitated knock he just looked at Amanda and said, 'How did you know?'

She had to control an hysterical impulse to giggle and say, 'I'm psychic,' but, seeing how pale and strained he looked, she pulled herself together and replied briefly, 'I heard about Julian Tankerton's accident and knew Sir Oscar would need a replacement for his opera at the Northern Counties Festival. I'm here—in case you need me.'

Without another word he took her hand and drew her into the house. Then he led her through to the music room, where she was not surprised to find Warrender sitting at the table absorbed in examining a pile of manuscript.

'She's here,' said Lewis, still in that wondering voice.

'Good girl,' replied Warrender without even looking up. Then he went to the piano, played several pages, nodded with an approving air and said, 'Come here, Amanda. Sing this for me.'

She went to him at once and sang as he directed her. Once or twice he stopped her, made her go back and try a phrase or two in a different way, then at last he turned and addressed Lewis.

'You're still determined to have her do it?'

'Absolutely.'

'But I'm not.' Amanda spoke with quiet emphasis.

'If you think someone else would be better, Sir Oscar, I'd prefer you to have her. I love the role, and I'd do my very best in it. But unless I would be the right person I don't want it.'

Lewis started to speak, but Warrender raised his hand in a gesture of complete authority which compelled silence.

'I think,' he said, addressing Amanda exclusively, 'that you probably *are* the best person. Were your development complete I would have no second thoughts about it. What we are having to gamble on is the fact that you are virtually a beginner, and how much Elsworth and I can put into you in the limited time available I just don't know.'

'I'm willing to gamble.' That was Lewis, pale and very determined.

'I don't doubt it, my dear fellow,' was the dry reply. 'But the principal gamble is mine. If the whole thing is a flop you are still an unknown composer who may do better one day. I, on the other hand, am staking my reputation as a conductor and organiser of some distinction. If I fail, my enemies—and they're many —will rejoice, while my friends will say uneasily, "Poor old Warrender, he's beginning to lose his touch." '

Recalling Jerome's malicious words the previous evening, Amanda winced. Then she said in a low but resolute tone of voice. 'Are you going to risk that, Sir Oscar?'

'Are you going to do exactly what I tell you for the next two and a half months?' he countered. And, taking her hand, he gave her the smile of infinite charm which he used only when it was essential for him to gain his point.

'I'm prepared to do anything and everything you

ask of me to the best of my ability,' she replied earnestly.

'Very well, we'll take the risk.' He got up from the piano. 'You'll drive back with me to London tonight. Lewis will find a substitute at the church here for the next few months and will join us tomorrow. By then I shall have gone through the whole score—' he gathered the manuscript sheets together in one comprehensive gesture—'and be ready to discuss any possible amendments. How about Rogerson?' He glanced at Lewis. 'Can we rely on his total collaboration in the coming weeks?'

'Entirely,' said Lewis and Amanda in one breath, and she added, 'He's staying at The Nightingale. I'll cycle back immediately and alert him. If you will stop for me on the way back, Sir Oscar, I'll have my things ready, and it's possible that he can come too. Oh——' she suddenly remembered her arrangement with Jeremy.

'What now?' Warrender asked a little impatiently.

'Nothing of any importance,' Amanda said in a tone of cool decision. And in that moment she knew she was speaking the exact truth. Jerome was no longer of any importance in her life. Indeed, she decided with a touch of malice in her turn, he deserved to be jettisoned if only for the disparaging way he had spoken of Sir Oscar the previous evening.

Lewis came with her to the front door, and in the narrow passage she turned and put her hands up against him.

'You're quite *sure* you want to gamble on me?' she said.

'There's no gamble involved,' he told her deliberately. 'We're going to succeed together. Why else do

you suppose I taught you to sing?' And he opened
the front door and ushered her out before she had
time to ask just what he meant by that.

On the way back she asked herself—did he mean
that he had had her in mind from the beginning to
be of use to him in his own career? Or did he mean
that this dramatic situation which linked them together seemed to him no more than the logical conclusion of all they had done together? She had found
no satisfactory reply by the time she reached The
Nightingale.

To Nan she explained rapidly that circumstances
forced her to go back to London earlier than she had
expected, and she asked her sister-in-law to telephone
Jerome and explain this. She herself felt unequal to
dealing with Jerome's inevitable questions, and she
was relieved when Nan agreed without any objection.

She did however ask curiously, 'Are you going
back by train?'

'No. Sir Oscar is calling for me in less than an
hour.—Oh, and Patrick too if he can manage it. It's
—it's all to do with the Northern Counties Festival,
but I don't know any details. And to tell the
truth—' as she saw several questions surfacing in
her sister-in-law's mind—'to tell the truth, Nan,
since you're going to tackle Jerome for me it's just as
well if you don't know too much. Then you can't
say anything out of turn.'

'Meaning—just be diplomatic and dumb?' Nan
suggested.

'Just that,' Amanda agreed with a smile. Then she
suddenly threw her arms round her sister-in-law and
exclaimed, 'Oh, Nan, say a prayer for me. I'm going
to need it in the coming weeks.'

'I will,' promised Nan quite seriously. 'And, what's

more, I won't ask questions. If Warrender himself has come to fetch you back it must be important. But I'm afraid Patrick will have to follow on his own. He went out only half an hour ago and said he wouldn't be in to dinner.'

'Did he say where he was going?' Amanda asked anxiously.

'No. Only that he'd be late.'

'Then get him to phone Lewis when he does come in—however late he is.'

'I will,' promised Nan, again controlling her desire to know more, but with obvious difficulty.

Amanda was ready and waiting with her suitcase packed ten minutes before Warrender arrived. He spared time for a few courteous enquiries after Henry, but then rapidly installed Amanda and her luggage in the car and, with a slight wave of his hand to Nan, set off towards London.

For quite a long time there was silence between them, Amanda feeling virtually certain that casual chit-chat would not be acceptable to her companion; certainly not when his thoughts were busy on something really important. She was surprised therefore when he remarked, 'You're very quiet. Are you worrying about what you're taking on? There's no need to do so—you'll be in safe hands.'

'Oh, I'm sure of that! My only worry is whether I'm really capable of doing justice to Lewis's work.'

'If I think at a later stage that you're not developing as we hope I shall have no scruples about replacing you,' he told her coolly.

'But Lewis can be so determined!'

'I too am not lacking in determination,' Warrender assured her. 'Take things one step at a time, and let me tell you that in the early stages you are essential.

You seem to have a very personal effect on Elsworth. Does he imagine he's in love with you?'

'Oh, no!' Amanda sounded shocked, and he laughed.

'It does happen, you know,' he said carelessly. 'He wouldn't be the first struggling composer to think he's found his ideal in a personable girl with an excellent voice. Treat him lightly in these early stages, whatever your own feelings may be. We need to keep him happy. You can brush him off later if you want to—once we have the first performance successfully over.'

There was a deep and disapproving silence from Amanda. Then she gathered sufficient courage to say, 'That isn't a very nice thing to say, Sir Oscar.'

'But then I'm not a very nice man, Amanda,' he replied amusedly. 'In fact, where my art is concerned I'm a totally ruthless professional. The sentimental amateur has no place in my scheme of things.'

'I believe you,' said Amanda. Then she added more provocatively than she knew, 'Lady Warrender practically told me as much.'

'Oh? What did Anthea say about me?' he asked, still amused but with a touch of genuine curiosity.

Amanda shook her head, however, and refused to amplify her remarks. He on his side did not give her the satisfaction of asking further questions, and the rest of the journey was completed more or less in silence.

On their arrival Anthea came running out into the hall to greet them and, seeing Amanda with her husband, exclaimed, 'You brought her! Then is everything—all right?'

'Not exactly that.' He kissed her a trifle absently. 'Let's say that the signs are favourable, so far as I have had time to examine the work. It's good—perhaps very much more than good. We'll see when we begin serious work on it. Amanda is to play the heroine—on the insistence of Elsworth.'

'Oh, my dear——' she hugged Amanda, 'I'm so glad for you!'

'You might spare her some pity too,' observed Warrender. 'It's going to be hell for her in the coming weeks.'

'There's no need to frighten her,' retorted Anthea. 'It *will* mean terrific work and probably some heartache too, Amanda. But you'll look back on it afterwards as one of the great periods of your life. I know —I've lived through something similar. It's like climbing a mountain on hands and knees, but if you do make it and reach the top it's like standing on the roof of the world. And no one can ever take that first breathtaking moment from you.'

'Except that there'll be times when you slip downhill again and have to retrace a very weary way.' Warrender told her drily. 'But that's an artist's life,' he added with a shrug.

'I'll do my best,' Amanda said again. 'I can't do more.'

'What do you mean—you can't do more?' Warrender challenged her contemptuously. '*You dare not do less!* Your best is the very least I shall require of you.'

And during the next few weeks Amanda found that was all too true. The task itself was very close to her heart, for she loved Lewis's music, which lay well for her voice, and she felt some strange kinship with the girl she was trying to portray. The day-to-day work of making the part individually hers was not impossibly difficult. What was difficult was the necessity of reaching and maintaining Oscar War-render's standards.

She was glad of Patrick Rogerson's co-operation, for he cheered her with his good-humoured optimism, but Lewis seemed unable to give her the same sort of support. Never having previously had anything to do with a creator in the throes of creation, Amanda was puzzled and distressed that he was so often nervous, tense and unreasonable. Almost, she told herself despairingly at times, as though he regretted his determination to have her sing the role.

A good many tears were shed in the privacy of her room, but only once did she break down in front of the three men, and then it was in a scene which blew up with the suddenness and violence of a thunderstorm. Towards the end of a taxing and strenuous afternoon in the studio she found herself less and less able to understand just what it was that was required of her. Sir Oscar, who hardly ever raised his voice to her, turned at last from the piano and asked in a tone of cold exasperation, 'Don't you understand anything, or are you just sulking?'

'I'm trying,' she said frightenedly. 'If you aren't satisfied——'

'If *I'm* not satisfied?' he repeated in a tone of unexpected rage. 'Who could be satisfied with such an abject performance? How satisfied do you suppose Lewis is feeling as you massacre this excellent work of his?'

'Leave me out of it,' Lewis growled.

'We can't leave you out of it. It's to you that the girl owes everything, and it's time she did something in return. And it's no good crying, Amanda——' he added, which naturally made Amanda burst into tears, at which Lewis went to her and put his arms round her.

'Don't start pampering her at this stage, for God's sake,' said Warrender. 'What she needs is a bracing view of the situation as it really is. You owe Lewis your splendid training, the chance of a lifetime with this unique operatic role he insists on your having, and in your private life the fact that he's paid every-thing to give your brother——'

'Be quiet!' exclaimed Lewis so violently that even the angry Warrender stopped in his tracks.

But enough had been said for Amanda to raise her white face from Lewis's shoulder where she had hid-den it, and to ask in a curious, shaken voice, 'What does he mean—everything?'

'He's exaggerating,' Lewis told her curtly. But he did not meet her eyes and, suddenly pulling herself away from his clasp, she walked across the room until she stood within a couple of feet of Warrender.

'You tell me the truth,' she said, looking the in-timidating conductor straight in the eye, 'or I go out of here, and you can find another soprano to bully-rag. Did Lewis pay everything that was needed for Henry?'

There was a long silence. Then Warrender re-plied, 'I'm sorry. That was really Elsworth's secret which I had no right to disclose. But—yes. And now you know the sum total of your debt to him perhaps you will put your best into making a success of his work.'

'I believed I was already doing just that,' Amanda said slowly. 'I see now that I was wrong. Will you please go away, both of you. Give me ten minutes to myself, and I'll be ready to go on.'

'I'd like to say——' began Lewis, but she rounded on the two of them and was astounded to hear herself shouting at them.

'Get out—both of you,' she ordered. 'And when you come back if I can't do everything you want I'll resign the part.'

To her astonishment they both went. And only when she heard the door close behind them did she realise that she had ordered Sir Oscar Warrender out of his own studio and he had gone.

She sat down then on a property couch and buried her face in her hands, though there were no longer any tears. She was just forcing herself to think and think. Not about the shattering discovery of the fullness of her debt to Lewis: strangely enough, she contrived to shut her mind off from that for the time being. What she thought about was the girl she was trying to portray, and why it was that she had been unable to absorb and apply what Sir Oscar had been telling her.

Deliberately she made her mind go blank. Then she slowly began to build up the scene again, with Warrender's words in the background of her consciousness. He had demanded what he called 'the colour of tears' in her voice, and suddenly she knew what he meant. She went over to the piano, fingered a note or two, cleared the huskiness from her throat and softly sang the phrases again.

She was still trying them over when the door opened and she switched round, ready to tell either Sir Oscar or Lewis that she had found what she needed. But it was not either of the men. It was Anthea Warrender, and she wheeled in a tea trolley set for two.

'You're probably in need of a cup of tea,' she

observed in a perfectly normal tone of voice.

'Did they tell you I—I made a scene?' Amanda asked.

'No. But they both looked rather chastened,' replied Anthea, 'and said you'd sent them out. I was so intrigued at the idea of anyone dismissing Oscar from his own studio that I felt you deserved—and probably needed—a cup of tea.'

'Thank you.' Amanda laughed shakily. 'I told them I wanted ten minutes to myself.'

'Oscar seemed to think half an hour would be better. And if you ask me, he was thinking of them as well as you.' Anthea poured out the tea and handed a cup to Amanda. 'Do you want to tell me what happened? or do you prefer to put it right out of your mind?'

'I couldn't do that,' Amanda said with a shake of her head. 'But if I answer your question will you then answer something for me?'

'If I can.'

So Amanda described the scene which had taken place and was relieved when the other girl nodded sympathetically and said, 'I'm sorry, my dear. I know how you must have felt. But it's no good my telling you to take no notice, because of course it's by taking full notice of these occasional miseries that we learn what to do.'

'Yes, I think I did learn what Sir Oscar meant, and I'm pretty sure I can do it now,' Amanda acknowledged unexpectedly. 'And will you please tell me in return—*why* did you let Lewis shoulder all the financial burden of helping Henry?'

'Oh—' Anthea bit her lip doubtfully—'so you know that was what happened?'

'Yes. It came out in the course of the—row.' Even

now she hesitated to apply that word to any scene
which involved Anthea's husband.

'Well, Amanda, it was mostly because he simply
wouldn't hear of anything else. He satisfied us that
he could manage it without real financial embarrassment, and beyond that point we could hardly
insist without offence.'

'But why did he *want* it that way?'

'I couldn't say for certain. But I think he regards
you very much as his creation, musically speaking,
and possibly he wanted to complete what one might
call a labour of love.'

'You don't think he wanted to put me under an
obligation to him, so that he would have some—some
sort of hold over me?'

'No, I don't.' Anthea shook her head slowly. 'Some
men would do that, of course. Heaven forgive me, I
once thought it of Oscar. But I was wrong. And I
think you would be wrong in attributing anything so
—so petty to Lewis. Besides, there was another
reason. He felt very deeply for your sister-in-law in
her distress, you know, and——'

'She had that impression too,' Amanda interrupted
quickly. 'He told her he knew what it meant to love
someone who was desperately ill and not be able to
do a thing about it.'

'Then you know about the young cousin?'

'The—cousin? It was a cousin, was it? How old
was she?'

'He,' corrected Anthea absently. 'Just a schoolboy,
I think, when he died.'

'So he—died?' Amanda's voice shook slightly, but
she could not have said whether this was because the
pathos of the story moved her or because she was

suddenly overwhelmed by some inexplicable sense of relief.

Anthea nodded. 'Apparently at the time Lewis had very little money and could do pathetically little for this boy to whom he was devoted. When he was telling us about it he said something I'll always remember because it was so true and so touching. He said nothing is easier to give than money if you have it—or more difficult if you have not. I think perhaps he felt that in helping your sick brother he was somehow doing what he'd longed fruitlessly to do for his own young cousin.'

There was quite a long silence. Then Amanda said, 'I'm sorry I said that about wondering if he wanted to put me under an obligation to him. It was quite unworthy. Of course he's far too generous to think of any such thing.'

'I agree.' Anthea got up and piled the tea things on the trolley once more. 'Shall I tell them they can come back now?'

'Yes, of course.' Amanda smiled suddenly. 'Sir Oscar may return to his own studio, and I'll somehow manage to do exactly what he wants of me.'

And she did. No one apologised to anyone else, though they were all specially polite to each other. Most remarkable of all, when Amanda did manage to do exactly what was required of her, Warrender refrained from asking her why she could not have done that before. There was never again anything approaching a real 'scene' between them. And by the time they all went north, to the lovely place in the Tyne Valley where the Northern Counties Festival took place every autumn, there was, on the surface at least, an atmosphere of artistic harmony. If they

all knew at heart that they were engaged on an unusually risky enterprise they did not discuss the fact.

By now there was a certain amount of press speculation about the new opera by a totally unknown
composer; and the equally unknown soprano who
was to sing the leading role came in for some notice
too. Warrender kept Amanda very much in the background, discouraging anything in the nature of inter-
views, saying the time for those would be when she
had made the grade.

As they all were guests in the big country house
from which the Festival was organised he was able
to keep a firm hand on Amanda and dictate almost
every detail of her daily life. With Lewis he was
naturally in a less authoritative position. But Lewis
himself seemed only too willing to remain out of the
direct limelight until the great first night should be
over.

During all this time Amanda had made no further
attempt to question him about his involvement in
her personal affairs. Only when Nan wrote to say
that Henry was coming home in a couple of weeks—
if not completely restored to health at least with the
confident expectation that he would be so in time—
she handed the letter to Lewis, and said, 'I think this
concerns you as much as us.'

She watched him while he read it and she saw the
colour come and go in his face. Even when she knew
he must have reached the end he did not look up
immediately, and she had the curious impression
that he was nervous and was at a loss for the right
words in which to make any comment.

This reversal of their usual roles touched her to
such a degree that she gently took the letter from

him, kissed his cheek and just said, 'Thank you, Lewis.'

'That's all right,' he replied a little awkwardly. 'There's nothing to thank me for. But I'm very glad about it.'

'So are we all. I'll tell you *how* glad when the first night is over.'

He did not query that, for by now it seemed to everyone concerned that all life was leading up to that great evening on which so much depended.

The dress rehearsal went well, giving Amanda a feeling of relative security about the task on which she was engaged. But when she awoke on the morning of the performance she was immediately aware of the most frightful sinking of the heart. Any confidence she had ever had seemed to have drained out of her, leaving her to wonder what insane impulse had prompted her to engage in this appalling gamble.

During the morning she reached the desperate conclusion that she must opt out entirely and leave the task to her understudy—an experienced artist a good deal older than herself and surely, surely much better fitted to do justice to Lewis's lovely work?

Pale and determined she finally went in search of Lewis. But in the big panelled hall she ran into Warrender, who looked at her, took her lightly by the arm and said, 'I know exactly how you're feeling. Come with me and let me talk to you for a few minutes.'

'You can't know how I'm feeling,' she muttered as he led her into their private sitting room and made her sit down. 'How could you? You're famous and secure, while I'm only the idiot of a girl who has just let herself be talked into an impossible task.'

'I also had a first performance,' he reminded her with a smile. Then he said, slowly and with considerable emphasis, 'Amanda, I seldom offer praise until a performance is safely over. But just because this is your first performance I'm going to tell you that in my judgment—which is a very good one—you are probably the *only* person who can do full justice to this unique role which Lewis has created.'

'But why? I'm totally inexperienced and sick with nervousness!'

'You're right to be nervous—you wouldn't be an artist if you were not. But your very inexperience is one of your advantages in this role. You're portraying a girl who is unknowing, bewildered, groping for the truth. This would not be sufficient of course if you had not got in the background of your experience an impeccable vocal technique, taught you by Lewis, and in charge of the performance probably the most experienced operatic conductor in the world,' he added almost carelessly.

She gave a shaky little laugh at that and said, 'With the last statement I entirely agree.'

'Then you may believe the rest. For if I may say so without false modesty—I *know*. You are the one person who can make an instant success of Lewis's work—so long as you do not yield to your own cowardice.'

Amanda sat up and unconsciously squared her shoulders.

'You mean that? You don't in your heart think that perhaps someone more experienced would do it better?'

'If I had thought that, my dear, I should have replaced you before now,' he told her drily. 'Lewis Elsworth's future is quite possibly in your hands.

Don't think of your future only. Think about his. If you love him——'

'If I—what?' Again she laughed unsteadily.

'All right. If you only like him—if you feel no more than grateful to him for all he has done—call on your courage, do your utmost as you have been taught during these many weeks, and leave the rest to me.'

He held out both hands to her and slowly she put hers into that firm, strong clasp which had, metaphorically speaking, upheld many a nervous performer long before Amanda had learned to sing a scale.

'I will succeed,' she said resolutely, and was unaware that the difference between that assertion and her first tentative, 'I'll do my best,' represented the completeness of her development under Warrender's tuition.

She felt almost tranquil for the rest of the day. And when Lewis came to her in her dressing-room to wish her luck before the performance, it was she who said to him, 'Don't be nervous. Remember, you said we were going to succeed together, and we *are*.'

'Darling——' he took her face between his hands and kissed her on the lips. Then suddenly, as though recalling some barrier he had inadvertently breached, he released her abruptly and went from the room. Amanda looked after him, faintly chilled by the curtness of his departure, but indefinably warmed by the way he had addressed her.

'He called me "darling",' she told herself. 'He never called me that before.' And though she forced herself to put that thought to the back of her consciousness for the rest of the evening, it was that word—and the sure hand of Oscar Warrender—

which sustained her from the first note to the last.

That was the only part of her which had anything to do with Amanda Lovett. For the rest of the time she was the strange, elusive, elemental creature who was struggling out of the darkness into the light. And, as Oscar Warrender had said, it was her essential inexperience and uncertainty which made the impersonation riveting. When she came to the almost primitive prayer to be saved from the Evil One, the deathly silence in the auditorium was the measure of the effect she created.

'That,' Warrender told his wife afterwards, 'was the moment when I knew she had made it.'

To Amanda herself the stunning awareness that she had made it came only with the final fall of the curtain and the almost bewildering ovation she received. Half frightened, she took one curtain call after another—with her colleagues, with Warrender and, finally, amid insistent calls for the composer, with Lewis. Then he left her alone on the stage and, looking out into the now lighted house, she saw Max Arrowsmith leaning on the orchestra rail and applauding enthusiastically, and she thought, 'None of this is really happening.'

In her tremulous joy she smiled uncertainly at him, and saw him make a gesture of complete approval before the curtains came together again. Then she left the stage to Lewis and his personal ovation, as the man principally responsible for what everyone clearly agreed was a great occasion.

When he came from the stage and found her in the wings he put his arm round her and went with her towards her dressing-room. Then in the narrow corridor outside the room he took both her hands and turned her to face him.

'I want to tell you——' he began. But suddenly, looking over his shoulder, she saw the totally unexpected figure of Nan, and with her a tall sunburned man she had never again expected to see standing so entirely erect.

'Henry!' she cried—'*Henry!*' and almost pushing Lewis from her, she rushed into her brother's arms. 'Henry——' She was unable to do anything but repeat his name over and over again, while she tried, not entirely successfully, to keep back the happy, excited tears. He patted her back as though she were a child, kissed her once or twice and then handed her on to Nan's warm embrace. By the time Amanda turned to include Lewis in the scene he had gone.

'Where's Lewis? I didn't hear what it was he wanted to say,' she exclaimed distractedly. But other people were crowding in on her, demanding her attention, congratulating, questioning and in some odd way taking possession of her. Indeed, it was all Nan could do to rescue her and come with her into the dressing-room, where Amanda dropped down in front of the mirror, started absently to remove her make-up and continued to say, 'Nan, Lewis was saying something. I didn't even answer him.'

'It probably wasn't important,' Nan told her soothingly.

'It was *terribly* important. I know it was!' Amanda sounded almost querulous and Nan too patted her as though she were a child, which illogically made Amanda even more distressed. And when Anthea came in a few minutes later she cut across any congratulations with the one, almost frantic question, '*Where is Lewis?*'

'In Oscar's room.' Anthea looked surprised.

'I must go to him.' Ignoring any objections from

the other two, she flung on her wrap and went out
into the corridor, where she found she had to push
her way though a crowd of delighted wellwishers
who sought to bar her way.

'Excuse me—oh, thank you—excuse me—yes, of
course I'm delighted—excuse me—how kind of you
—excuse——'

At last she stood before the conductor's door and,
rapping peremptorily, she went in even before Warrender's voice bade her enter. He was sitting in shirt-
sleeves, putting some splendid diamond links in his
cuffs. But Amanda had no eyes for him—or his cuff-
links. She went straight to the other figure in the
room and said urgently,

'Lewis, what was it you were going to say to me?
I didn't mean to push you aside—it was my joy and
surprise at seeing Henry. I wanted him to speak to
you—to thank you himself, but you were gone. What
was it you meant to say to me?'

'Just that there was no question of thanks any
more. That you need never, never again think you
were under any sort of obligation, because tonight
you made me a success. I'm free! That damned
weight is gone and——'

'What damned weight?' She looked up at him in
puzzled dismay. 'It's *I* who had the weight of obligation if anyone did.'

'But that was it; that was what coloured our whole
relationship. There was not a thing I could say to
you or ask you without the blight of your insisting
that you owed me too much to make an impersonal
decision. Even Warrender was ass enough to
say——'

'At the risk of being an ass enough to say the
wrong thing again—' Warrender's cool voice sud-

denly reminded them that they were not alone—'I apologise for taking part quite involuntarily in this scene, but this does happen to be my dressing-room. However, if you will be patient three minutes longer—' he reached for his jacket and shrugged himself into it—'I will leave you in full possession.'

'I'm so sorry,' exclaimed Amanda and Lewis in chastened chorus.

'No, no, don't be sorry,' Warrender strapped on his wrist watch and swept some odd coins into his pocket. 'You chose the scene rather well, as a matter of fact, for your confusing and confused conversation had a salutary touch of nostalgia for an old stager like myself.' He paused and looked thoughtfully at them both. 'Perhaps one should not give advice to young people, except professionally, but—' he shrugged slightly—'it is now many years since I discovered the profound truth that between people who love each other there should be no argument about who owes whom, or how to balance out this or that. That is for people who do not love each other. They of course can argue academically about these things for hours.'

He wound a white muffler round his throat and took down his overcoat. Then at the door he turned and smiled at them. 'I'm expecting you to join us for supper in half an hour. If you don't arrive, I shall know you are still arguing.'

Then he went out of the room, to the confused chorus of, 'Sir Oscar, could I have your autograph?' 'Sir Oscar, if you would just——'

The door closed, shutting out the rest of the world, so far as Amanda and Lewis were concerned.

'I love you,' he said before she could. 'I've loved you almost since I first heard you sing "Hear ye,

Israel". I would have told you so long, long ago, my little Amanda, if I hadn't been so afraid that your sense of obligation would confuse your real feelings.'

'How silly of you, darling. How absolutely idiotic of you,' replied Amanda fondly, and she put her arms round his neck and kissed him. 'You just made things unnecessarily difficult. It took me much longer than it need have to discover that I loved you. You were so—so *discouraging*, Lewis!'

He laughed at that, much more heartily and uninhibitedly than she had ever heard him laugh before. Then he kissed her and began to say, 'If you only knew——' but Warrender's dresser looked in and said, 'Oh, Sir Oscar——'

'It's all right,' Lewis told him gaily, as he glanced round evidently thinking he had mistaken the room. 'Sir Oscar just went out ahead of us.' And he ushered Amanda into the corridor, where several people were still hanging about.

'Would you *please* sign my programme?' An earnest-looking schoolgirl thrust her programme into Amanda's hand. 'I've waited so long. And this is my first time ever at the opera.'

'Oh, my dear!' Suddenly Amanda felt gloriously grown-up and experienced and professional. 'It's my first opera too—and the first time anyone has ever asked me for my autograph. I'm sorry I kept you waiting.'

'We're both sorry,' said Lewis behind her, and there was a note of happy laughter in his voice. 'But, you see, we were getting engaged.'

Here's how to get your volume NOW!

MAIL IN	$	GET
2 SPECIAL PROOF-OF-PURCHASE SEALS*	PLUS $1 U.S.	ONE BOOK
5 SPECIAL PROOF-OF-PURCHASE SEALS*	PLUS 50¢ U.S.	ONE BOOK
8 SPECIAL PROOF-OF-PURCHASE SEALS*	FREE	ONE BOOK

*Special proof-of-purchase seal from inside back cover of all specially marked Harlequin "Let Your Imagination Fly Sweepstakes" volumes. No other proof-of-purchase accepted.

ORDERING DETAILS:

Print your name, address, city,

PLEASE PRINT

Name

Address

Apt. No.

City

State/ Prov.

Zip/Postal Code

Let Your Imagination Fly Sweepstakes

Rules and Regulations:

NO PURCHASE NECESSARY

1. Enter the Let Your Imagination Fly Sweepstakes 1, 2 or 3 as often as you wish. Mail each entry form separately bearing sufficient postage. Specify the sweepstake you wish to enter on the outside of the envelope. Mail a completed entry form or, your name, address, and telephone number printed on a plain 3"x 5" piece of paper to:

HARLEQUIN LET YOUR IMAGINATION FLY SWEEPSTAKES,

P.O. BOX 1280, MEDFORD, N.Y. 11763 U.S.A.

2. Each completed entry form must be accompanied by 1 Let Your Imagination Fly proof-of-purchase seal from the back inside cover of specially marked Let Your Imagination Fly Harlequin books (or the words "Let Your Imagination Fly" printed on a plain 3" x 5" piece of paper. Specify by number the Sweepstakes you are entering on the outside of the envelope.

3. The prize structure for each sweepstake is as follows:

Sweepstake 1 - North America

Grand Prize winner's choice: a one-week trip for two either Bermuda; Montreal, Canada; or San Francisco. 3 Grand Prizes will be awarded (min. approx. retail value $1,375. U.S., based on Chicago departure) and 4,000 First Prizes: scarves by nik nik, worth $14. U.S. each. All prizes will be awarded.

Sweepstake 2 - Caribbean

Grand Prize winner's choice: a one-week trip for two to either Nassau, Bahamas; San Juan, Puerto Rico; or St. Thomas, Virgin Islands. 3 Grand Prizes will be awarded. (Min. approx. retail value $1,650. U.S., based on Chicago departure) and 4,000 First Prizes: simulated diamond pendants by Kenneth Jay Lane, worth $15. U.S. each. All prizes will be awarded.

Sweepstake 3 - Europe

Grand Prize winner's choice: a one-week trip for two either London, England; Frankfurt, Germany; Paris, France; or Rome, Italy. 3 Grand Prizes will be awarded. (Min. approx. retail value $2,800. U.S., based on Chicago departure) and 4,000 First Prizes: 1/2 oz. bottles of perfume, BLAZER by Anne Klein (Retail value over $30. U.S.). All prizes will be awarded.

Grand trip prizes will include coach round-trip airfare for two persons from the nearest commercial airport serviced by Delta Air Lines to the city as designated in the prize, double occupancy accommodation at a first-class or medium hotel, depending on vacation, and $500. U.S. spending money. Departure taxes, visas, passports, ground transportation to and from airports will be the responsibility of the winners.

4. To be eligible, Sweepstakes entries must be received as follows:

Sweepstake 1 Entries received by February 28, 1981
Sweepstake 2 Entries received by April 30, 1981
Sweepstake 3 Entries received by June 30, 1981
Make sure you enter each Sweepstake separately since entries will not be carried forward from one Sweepstake to the next.

The odds of winning will be determined by the number of entries received in each of the three sweepstakes. Canadian residents, in order to win any prize, will be required to first correctly answer a time-limited skill-testing question, to be posed by telephone, at a mutually convenient time.

5. Random selections to determine Sweepstake 1, 2 or 3 winners will be conducted by Lee Krost Associates, an independent judging organization whose decisions are final. Only one prize per family, per sweepstake. Prizes are non-transferable and non-refundable and no substitutions will be allowed. Winners will be responsible for any applicable federal, state and local taxes. Trips must be taken during normal tour periods before June 30, 1982. Reservations will be on a space-available basis. Airline tickets are non-transferable, non-refundable and non-redeemable for cash.

6. The Let Your Imagination Fly Sweepstakes is open to all residents of the United States of America and Canada, (excluding the Province of Quebec) except employees and their immediate families of Harlequin Enterprises Ltd., its advertising agencies, Marketing & Promotion Group Canada Ltd. and Lee Krost Associates, Inc., the independent judging company. Winners may be required to furnish proof of eligibility. Void wherever prohibited or restricted by law. All federal, state, provincial and local laws apply.

7. For a list of trip winners, send a stamped, self-addressed envelope to:

Harlequin Trip Winners List, P.O. Box 1401, MEDFORD, N.Y. 11763 U.S.A.

Winners lists will be available after the last sweepstake has been conducted and winners determined.

NO PURCHASE NECESSARY